ONE MINUTE PAST EIGHT

The headquarters of Segurnal—*short for Seguridad Na-*
cional, and sometimes known as the secret police—was the
last place Jeff Lane had expected to be his first night in
Caracas.

He'd arrived earlier that evening and had gone directly
to the Hotel Tucan to meet Baker, the private detective
who'd cabled he'd found Arnold Grayson, but by that time
Baker could no longer talk. Grayson however was there at
Segurnal too, still as antagonistic as he had been four years
before, but still uncommitted, despite the trick at the
Miami Airport which had cost Jeff twelve hours and had
given Karen Holmes an all-important lead over him.

For Jeff and Karen it was to become a game of cat-and-
mouse in a strange land among strange people. There
were, for instance, Pedro Vidal, head man of Segurnal;
Carl Webb, hood, gambler, and collection-man for a
missing hundred and twenty thousand dollars; Muriel Mi-
randa, who had the height to complement her curves, but
not the depth to restrain her dreams; and Julio Cordovez,
soft-spoken, good friend, and perhaps the most dangerous
of all.

The cat usually catches the mouse. How it does so—and
when—is more often the heart of the matter. Rarely has
George Harmon Coxe written more excitingly, with more
pace and action, and with more atmospheric evocation,
than in this story of greed and murder in South America.

GEORGE HARMON COXE

One
Minute Past Eight

ALFRED · A · KNOPF NEW YORK

© GEORGE HARMON COXE, 1957

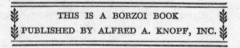

THIS IS A BORZOI BOOK
PUBLISHED BY ALFRED A. KNOPF, INC.

FOR
SUSAN

ONE MINUTE PAST EIGHT

1

IN THE beginning Jeff Lane did not know it was a pick-up. That the idea never crossed his mind was not due to his ignorance of either the technique or the procedure, nor was his Bostonian background or any latent streak of Puritanism a contributing factor. He had been accosted on the street on occasion in the early hours, and women of various ages and inclinations had made opening gambits when perched on near-by bar stools. In this instance it was not the circumstances that fooled him, it was the girl herself.

What made it easier was the fact that this particular New York—Miami flight was no more than half full. For Jeff had been assigned an aisle scat on this afternoon in mid-March and his seat-mate was a red-faced fat man whose bulk extended laterally and put a noticeable pressure on Jeff's arm and shoulder. As a result, when the passenger warning on the bulkhead winked off, he made his way forward to the unoccupied section and pre-empted a window seat.

When he had adjusted the air vents and got a cigarette going he opened his magazine, thumbing idly through it and glancing out the window as the aircraft climbed and the earth receded. Sometime later—he had not yet begun to concentrate on his reading—the girl went by on her way to the forward rest-rooms and as he appraised her figure from the rear, he knew that this was the same girl who had stood next to him at the ticket counter at Idlewild.

At the time he had been concentrating on his own problems—he wanted to be sure that when he changed planes in Miami his bags would be automatically checked on through to Caracas—but even so he was conscious of a faint odor of gardenias and the impression remained that this girl was both smart and attractive. Now he saw that she was rather tall, that the seams on her nylons were straight, that she moved gracefully even on the high heels. Her tailored suit was a medium gray with a short jacket that lay flat against the neat hips; the piece of felt, hardly larger than a cap, that topped her mahogany-colored hair was dark red, and the leather bag under her arm matched it.

Minutes later some movement caught the corner of his eye and he glanced up to see her coming down the aisle. He got a quick picture of her, enough to know that she was equally attractive from the front, and then, as he started to look away, she smiled. It was a nice friendly smile, surprising him a little so that he was slow to react, and suddenly he realized she was going to speak to him.

The very fact that she took the initiative both flustered and flattered him, and as she stopped with one hand on the top of the seat in front he saw that she had a lovely complexion, that her well-spaced eyes were dark blue, that the odor he had noticed came from two gardenias pinned to her jacket.

"Hello," she said. "You were next to me at the counter in New York."

"I remember," Jeff said.

"I heard you talking about Caracas and I wondered if—" She paused and smiled again. "Do you mind if I—"

She leaned down to remove the crossed seat belts and Jeff pulled himself erect. "Here," he said. "Sit by the window."

He stepped into the aisle as she protested. "I just wanted to stop a minute. You'd probably rather read your magazine."

"I'd rather talk to you," Jeff said.

"Well"—she slid in front of him and settled herself in the seat—"all right. When I start to bore you I'll go quietly." She put her bag in her lap and glanced out the window before she looked at him. "I've never been in Caracas," she said, "and I don't speak much Spanish and I thought you might be able to tell me what to expect. Have you been there before—I hope?"

"Once," Jeff said and chuckled. "One full day, from a cruise ship that stopped at La Guaira. But that was five years ago and I understand there've been a lot of changes."

"Do you know Spanish?"

"About ten words."

"Oh . . . Well, do you think one can get by without it?"

Jeff said he thought so; at least in Caracas. "Are you on a holiday?"

"For two weeks. I have a brother who works for one of the oil companies. In Carapita. I think I came down on the plane with you from Boston," she added, digressing. "Is that your home?"

"Yes," Jeff said. "I'm Jeffrey Lane."

"Karen Holmes," she said and smiled again. "How do you do? Are you on holiday too?"

Jeff said no. He said this was just a quick business trip and he did not expect to be in Caracas more than two or three days.

"Lane?" she said as if testing the word. "Would that be the Lane Manufacturing Company in Cambridge?"

Jeff said yes, a little surprised that she should have heard of it, and then asked her where she lived in Boston. They were unable to find any mutual friends but as the plane droned on in the sunshiny world above the blanket of clouds he learned that she had gone to Wellesley and was working as a secretary in one of the insurance companies.

A second glance at the smart sharkskin suit and its accessories told him she must be a first-class secretary and it gave him an odd sense of satisfaction to note that she wore no ring. He noted, too, that in certain lights there was a coppery sheen to her hair, that in profile her lashes would need no mascara, and that her red mouth was softly humorous. Because she was so easy to talk to he found himself telling her he had gone to Cornell and Harvard Business School and that except for two years in Korea he had always worked in the family business, during the summers as a youngster and then, after graduation, moving in to learn the business. He did not add that he was one of the three vice presidents, at twenty-nine, nor that, now that his father was dead, he would some day be president, provided George Tyler of the Tyler-Texas Corporation failed in his present concerted effort to get control of the company.

This was something he had been thinking about most of his waking hours during the past days, and now he deliberately put the matter from his mind. For the moment it was enough that he had a pretty companion, and he enjoyed their effortless conversation until he noticed the sun was beginning to settle in the west. This told him it was nearly time for a drink.

"What would you like?" he asked.

"Oh, dear, I don't know." She glanced at her wristwatch. "Could I have a raincheck? Could I wait until we get to Miami? As a matter of fact I was going to suggest it then anyway. . . . But you go ahead if you like."

He grinned at her and said he could wait. He said there was a place in the terminal and maybe that was a good idea. "I hadn't realized we were nearly there," he said, and

then, as if to corroborate the statement, one of the steward-
esses claimed their attention over the loudspeaker.

They would be landing in twenty minutes, she said,
and she wished to remind them to take all personal be-
longings with them when they left the aircraft.

"Passengers continuing on to Curaçao and Caracas will
have a wait of approximately an hour," she added. "The
flight will be announced over the loudspeaker system but
please stay within the terminal building so the announcement can be heard. Thank you."

The International Airport was a busy place at that hour.
A plane was loading as Jeff accompanied the girl toward
the incoming gate, another was taxiing for take-off. Two
were gliding in for landings, the more distant one making
its final turn toward the assigned runway. A dozen more
silent aircraft stood in a row, their noses slanting obliquely
toward the terminal building; refueling crews were busy,
and baggage trucks crisscrossed on the concrete behind
their midget tractors.

The humid breeze made his winter suit feel heavy, and
once inside the building Jeff headed toward the bar and
restaurant near the street side. About halfway there he felt
the girl's hand on his arm and when he turned she gestured at the two blue-canvas flight bags he was carrying.

"If you'll give me mine," she said, "and five minutes
while I fix my face, I'll meet you by the entrance."

Jeff said all right and released her bag. When she started
off he hesitated a moment and then headed for the men's
room. Here he hung up his trench coat, slipped out of his
jacket, and rolled up his sleeves. He washed his hands and
face, rubbed wet hands over his dark hair, which was cut
rather short and did not need much combing. As he stood
drying his hands he was a moderately tall man with a
lanky look, and his flat-muscled body moved with an easy
co-ordination which might have come from hours of drudg-

ery pulling the number-seven oar on a junior-varsity shell
during his college days. His brows were straight above
dark-brown eyes which somehow reflected a sense of humor, as did the full easy mouth. His face was too bony to
be called handsome, but he had more than average good
looks, and now, thinking of Karen Holmes and the journey
yet to come, a smile worked at the corners of his mouth
and his eyes had the look of a man well pleased with himself.

When he realized he was daydreaming, he threw the
towel into the wire basket, donned his jacket, and went
back into the waiting-room. A glance at the glass doors of
the restaurant told him he was early, and as he started
toward them his eyes searched the room to his right. For a
moment he thought he saw the dark red hat flanked by
two men who were earnestly talking to its owner. Then a
chattering family group moved in front of him, blocking
his view. He was standing beside the door when he saw her
coming, moving quickly on slender, well-shaped legs.

Not really looking at him, she muttered something about
hoping she had not kept him waiting, and then they were
inside, finding a small table opposite the bar.

"Scotch, I think," she said when he had asked what she
would like. "I might even have a double if I can have it in a
large glass. . . . Do you think they'll feed us on the plane?"

Jeff realized that the light had begun to fade and saw
that it was nearly seven o'clock. He said: "They'll have to
feed us," and gave the waitress the order, wondering now
if there had been some change in the girl's manner or
whether it was his imagination. She had not yet looked
him directly in the eyes and her hands were never still as
they opened and closed her bag, adjusted the paper doily
the waitress had left, and moved the ashtray to one side.
Twice she touched the turned-up ends of her hair, and
now her glance moved restlessly about the room, as if some

inner tension was working on her that had been totally
absent on the plane. The arrival of the drinks claimed his
attention and he glanced at the check and put a bill on it.
Then he saw that she was fumbling in her bag again and
asked if she wanted a cigarette.

"I have some, thanks," she said, and now she brought
forth some silver. "But I wonder if you would get me a
couple of packs from the machine. I understand they're
expensive in Caracas."

"Sure," Jeff said. "Let *me* get them."

"No, really," she said and pressed the coins into his hand.
"Chesterfield regulars, please."

He pushed back his chair and went to the vending machine near the door, stopping to read the card and see
how much was needed. He had enough change for four
packs and he gave three of them to her when he sat down
again.

"Well," he said, realizing for the first time how thirsty
he was and lifting his glass, "to a pleasant flight."

"And a safe one," she said, her small smile automatic
and something in her eyes he could not understand, a shad-
owy something that seemed in that instant almost more like
fear than nervousness.

Then her glance focused on her glass and she took a
sip while Jeff swallowed three times, fast, and was glad
she had thought to suggest a double.

"That tastes good," he said when she lowered her glass
and took a cigarette from the pack he had put on the table.
He gave her a light and looked idly about, refusing to speculate further on the sudden change in her mood.

He heard her ask where he would be staying and he
said: "The Tucan. Will your brother be meeting you?"

"No. He can't get in until the following day. I—I'll be
at the Tucan too."

He finished his drink and put the glass down, again

aware of the uncomfortable heaviness of his suit. The static-like sounds in the room—the buzz of conversation, the clatter of glasses and dishes—were less distinct now and his face felt hot. He took a deep breath and when he looked across the table the girl's face seemed to waver like a television image not quite in focus. Only her eyes seemed intent and watchful and from out of the distance he heard her speak.

"Is it stuffy in here, or is it just me?"

"Stuffy," he said, wondering why since the room was air conditioned. "Very stuffy."

"Then let's get out in the fresh air."

She pushed back her chair. He reached for the flight bags and nearly fell over, and then he lurched to his feet, staggering a little before he caught his balance and thinking:

This is ridiculous. Why should a double Scotch hit me like this? "I'm sorry," he said, his voice sounding curiously remote in his ears. "I'll be O. K. in a minute."

Somehow he got through the glass doors and now the floor was tilting and he felt her hand on his arm as she tried to steady him.

She said: "Let's go outside," and he felt himself walking. When he stopped he knew somehow that they were standing on the loading platform in the gathering dusk.

He could hear cars pull into the curbing and doors slam and baggage slide gratingly across the concrete. In the background the voices he heard no longer had any meaning. The urge to sit down and rest a minute was overwhelming now and he was vaguely conscious of firm hands supporting his arms. Men's voices throbbed close by and then he was stumbling along into space. Finally, as his eyes closed, he heard someone telling him to take it easy, to sit back and relax. The last thing he remembered was the distant slam of a car door.

2

IT WAS early when Jeff Lane woke the next morning. He could tell this from the amount of light that came in through the two windows, but it was a subconscious knowledge and it took a while for his mind to function properly. He understood first that he was in bed, apparently in a hotel room. A light blanket covered him and as he became aware of his body he knew that he was clad in shorts and undershirt.

The throbbing of his head and the thick disgusting taste in his mouth suggested a monumental hangover, but he could not remember how he got it. He knew he should be in Caracas, but he could recall nothing of the flight or his arrival at the hotel. Still groping mentally he raised his head and found his suit draped on a chair in front of the desk, the blue flight bag resting on the floor near by. His trench coat had been tossed on a second chair, but there was no sign of the two bags he had checked in Boston, and suddenly some silent alarm rang in his brain and he jumped out of bed and staggered over to the window.

The brightening of the sky told him the sun was coming up. Serried silhouettes of luxury hotels on the horizon stretched as far as he could see, and palm trees fringed the opposite shore of a bay crisscrossed with causeways and dotted with artificial islands. Only then did he know that the street below the window was Bayshore Drive and that he was looking at Biscayne Bay and Miami Beach; only then did his mind open up and let the memories come flooding back to compound the sickness that had heretofore been only physical. The answer that came to him left him staggered and incredulous, and now, a glance at his wristwatch telling him it was six twenty, he strode back to the bed and snatched up the telephone.

"Desk clerk," he said when the operator answered; then, seconds later: "Hello. This is Mr. Lane in"—he glanced at the circular disk on the pedestal—"1604. Were you on duty when I checked in last night?"

"Just a moment, please."

Another pause. Another voice.

"Hello, Mr. Lane. I was on the desk last night."

"What time did I come in?"

"About eight thirty. I can tell you exactly if you—"

"No, no!" Jeff said. "That's all right. Did I register?"

"I beg your pardon."

"Did I do the registering? Did I come in alone?"

"Oh, no. Two friends brought you, Mr. Lane. You—ah—what I mean is, you weren't able to register without help. You could hardly stand. Your friends said you'd been celebrating and—well, I took their word for it."

"One of them registered for me?"

"And paid for the room in advance."

"They came up to the room with me?"

"Yes. Someone had to. When they came back they said not to disturb you, that you'd be all right in the morning. They seemed very solicitous."

"Yeah," Jeff said, bitterness tingeing his words. "I'll bet."

He hung up and sat on the edge of the bed, his dark gaze brooding and morose, the object of his resentment a girl named Karen Holmes. He recalled her smartness, her nice complexion, the dark-blue eyes that had seemed so friendly and ingenuous. Every step of the clever routine came back to haunt him: the postponement of the drink on the plane, the suggestion of a double drink to make it less likely that he would notice the drug she had slipped into his glass after she had sent him to the cigarette machine. Here in Miami she had needed help—he remembered the two men he had thought he had seen talking to a woman in a dark-red hat—but until then she had done a letter-perfect job quite alone.

Because he now understood the reason for the pick-up, he stood up and went over to his coat. The wallet was in its customary pocket. The money in the bill compartment seemed intact. The birth certificate, the three copies of his tourist card, each with its passport-size photograph, were there. So was the cable that had started him on this trip.

It had been sent from Caracas by a man named Harry Baker, a private detective employed by the Lane Manufacturing Company for the past two months in an effort to find Jeff's stepbrother, who had dropped out of sight four years earlier. Now, unfolding the cable, which was a long one sent at the deferred rate, he read it again:

Your stepbrother Arnold living here under his father's name of Grayson listed in phone book. Have explained situation and requested return to Boston but Grayson holding up definite answer. Suggest you come earliest convenience to outline proposition in person. Feel my job done with this cable and am now off payroll. Have accepted temporary assignment here but will see you at Tucan where room engaged for you adjoining mine. Advise date of arrival. Baker.

The message had been sent on the previous Friday, but at the deferred rate it had not been delivered until Saturday morning. A quick conference of company officials voted to accept Baker's suggestion and elected Jeff to represent them, but it had taken all day Monday to arrange for his tourist cards. By that time the through flight from New York to Caracas was booked to capacity, and rather than wait for the through flight on Wednesday he had settled for the next best schedule.

Replacing the cable as his mind went on, he knew that Karen Holmes's mission was to delay him so that she could talk to his stepbrother first. He knew, too, that she must be working for the Tyler-Texas Corporation just as he knew that if Arnold Grayson decided to vote the shares he would presently claim as part of his stepfather's estate with the Tyler-Texas crowd, the Lane officials would presently lose control of the company.

But how could Karen Holmes know about the cable? How did she know what plane he was taking? Who were the men who helped her at the Miami airport? How could—

He broke off the thoughts abruptly, aware that such speculation was not only a waste of time but served also to aggravate his frustration and resentment. There were better things to do and now he went back to the bedside table and consulted the telephone directory. When he found the number of the airline he wanted he put in his call and explained the situation, saying that he had been taken ill at the airport the night before and missed the Caracas flight.

"What happens to the bags I checked through?" he said. "When can I get out of here?"

The airline clerk heard him out and then said: "Let me check on this, Mr. Lane. Where can I call you back, say in five minutes?"

Jeff told her and then went over to examine his flight bag, finding nothing missing and taking out his toilet kit and the clean shirt. He went into the bathroom to brush his teeth and by the time he had finished the telephone summoned him back to the bedroom.

"I've checked with the terminal office, Mr. Lane," the clerk said, "and there's no need to worry about your bags.

They'll be waiting at Maiquetia; that is if you plan to continue to Caracas."

"Good," Jeff said. "When can I get out of here?"

"We have a flight this morning at seven forty and another at eleven thirty."

"How much difference in time of arrival?"

"Only fifteen minutes. That's because the first flight goes by way of Camaguey, Kingston, Barranquilla, and Maracaibo; the later one goes to Port au Prince, Ciudad Trujillo, and Curaçao."

Jeff said he wasn't interested in scenery and was there a seat on the eleven-thirty flight.

"Yes, there is. Be at the airport at ten forty-five or at our downtown office at ten fifteen."

Jeff hung up, tickled the connection bar, and when he got the operator, asked for room service. He ordered tomato juice, toast, and a double order of coffee. While he waited he shaved and showered, the cold spray washing away some of his physical lassitude but doing very little to cure his internal queasiness.

When the waiter had been paid, tipped, and had taken his departure Jeff tried the black coffee and waited for it to hit the bottom of his stomach before he continued. When it stayed down he tried the juice and found it good. Thus encouraged he finally ate a piece of toast, not because he wanted it but because he thought he should. The second cup of coffee reassured him sufficiently to try a cigarette and by that time he knew he was going to be all right. . . .

As the DC 6-B winged its way east and south through the bright afternoon skies, Jeff Lane was in no mood to appreciate the view afforded him by his window seat. The Caribbean was blue as advertised except along the reefs of nameless islands. The spectacular mountains of Haiti and the Dominican Republic were no different from other wooded tropical mountains he had seen before, and the picturesqueness of Port au Prince became to him only a half-hour stop when, because of regulations, he had to leave the plane while it was refueled. Ciudad Trujillo meant a wait of twenty minutes, and after that there were only clouds and water below the wings and a torment in his mind as he thought of Karen Holmes and the Tyler-Texas Corporation, and of the man he had grown up to accept as Arnold Lane, now known as Arnold Grayson.

He, Jeff, had been four and his sister six when his father had married a widow named Grayson with an eleven-year-old son, and in the early years, Jeff's memory of Arnold was hazy. He understood now that his stepbrother was a bully with an ingrown streak of meanness which in those days revealed itself with a cuff, a pinch, or a twist of the arm, always surreptitious, so there would be no parental punishment.

Later he learned, from dinner-table talk, of Arnold's escapades at three prep schools before one tolerated him long enough for graduation. There had been a year each at two universities, followed by a series of jobs in and out of the family company. What made it more difficult for Jeff's father was the fact that he was devoted to his second wife, and while she was alive he overlooked her son's troublesome ways. It was only after she had died and Arnold was older that he seemed to realize the hopelessness of the obligation he had assumed.

Even so, he tried, and though these were the years that Jeff was in college and, later, in Korea, he knew of two occasions when only his father's help had kept Arnold from prison. The first came as a result of a bar-room brawl when Arnold had cut a man severely with a broken bottle. Influence and twenty thousand dollars to the injured man helped Arnold get off with a suspended sentence. The second case was one of out-and-out embezzlement from a

brokerage partnership that Jeff's father had financed originally. Here again the shortage was made up, but with this
came an ultimatum. From now on Arnold was on his own;
there would be no more money, no allowance, no hope of
any inheritance.

The ultimatum was delivered by registered letter to a
Los Angeles address where Arnold was staying four years
earlier. Jeff had not seen him since. He had heard Arnold
was in Las Vegas for a time and he knew that two men
from that city had come looking for him in Boston. He still
did not know why.

Yet, in the end, Jeff's father had relented. It may have
been some twist of conscience once he knew he was going
to die; it may have been due to the fact that he had once
loved Arnold's mother and still felt some obligation to her
son. Whatever the reason, he had called Jeff in to say he
had changed his will and that if Arnold could be found
within ninety days he was to share equally with Jeff's sister
and himself in the forty-five per cent of the Company
shares still held by the family.

Jeff had promised to do his best to locate Arnold, and
it was a promise he intended to keep, if possible, in spite
of this deep-rooted dislike of his stepbrother. And so Harry
Baker had been hired to try to pick up the trail, after four
years, a trail that led up and down the West Coast, to
Las Vegas, and back to Los Angeles, to Panama, and finally, with roughly thirty days to go before the bequest
would be invalidated, the search had ended with the cable
Jeff now carried in his pocket.

To claim his inheritance, Arnold Grayson had to return
to Boston, but once he claimed it he could vote his fifteen
per cent of the company stock as he saw fit. Somehow,
George Tyler of Tyler-Texas had learned about Jeff's mission, and Karen Holmes now had a twelve-hour start at

trying to convince Arnold to cast his lot with the opposition. . . .

The voice of the stewardess demanding attention cut through Jeff's thoughts and he listened as she announced the impending arrival of Flight 433 at Curaçao.

"We will be on the ground approximately thirty minutes," she said. "Passengers en route to Caracas may leave their personal things on the aircraft."

Jeff listened as the instructions were repeated in Spanish and then he looked out the window at things he had seen once before from the ground: the compact little city of Willemstad, the channel leading to the landlocked harbor, the oil tanks, the famous pontoon bridge which separated the two parts of the city and was constantly being opened and closed to make way for the coastal tankers that shuttled back and forth from Venezuela. As the plane banked again he saw that the bridge was open now, the municipal free ferry which served the populace angling toward the main part of town ahead of two oncoming tankers. Then the aircraft was dipping and he sat back to await the landing.

Flight 433 was twenty minutes early coming into Maiquetia, the modern airfield close by La Guaira, where the mountains of Venezuela level out on the man-made plateau before touching the sea. There were two terminals here, one for local traffic, the larger and more impressive structure serving international flights.

Once on the ground the passengers were herded together and ushered by an official past a patrolling FAK— a green-uniformed, tin-hatted, rifle-carrying member of the National Guard—to the small air-conditioned waiting-room which funneled the passengers in to the immigration authorities.

Because he was in a hurry, Jeff had managed to be second in line, and now he stood before one of two clerks who began to fill in cards on their typewriters. He showed his papers, answered questions automatically, and was finally instructed to come behind the counter to a pair of desks near the end of the room.

Here he stood before a mustached, grim-faced individual, who inspected his tourist cards and birth certificate, inspected him personally and with some care, and then consulted two bulky loose-leaf black books. Apparently there was some cross-indexing involved, because it took a while and pages were flipped one way and then the other in an effort to find out if one Jeffrey Lane had anything against his name or record that would make him undesirable as a tourist. Jeff guessed that the procedure was more of a safeguard for political reasons than anything else, so he stood and waited until the man flipped his papers with a weary gesture to the adjoining desk. A second official stamped the three tourist cards, initialed them, gave one to Jeff along with the birth certificate, and put the other two aside.

"Keep," he said, and nodded him out past the counters and toward the customs room.

Jeff reclaimed his two bags, which were already there, unlocked them, watched them chalk-marked, and then stood aside as a porter snatched them from the counter and led the way out of the air-conditioned pleasantness into the humid warmth of the early evening. There was still some afterglow in the sky, but here the lights had been turned on and presently he was relaxing in the back seat of a late-model car.

"Hotel Tucan," he said and from over his shoulder the driver said: "*Sí.*"

Minutes later they were on the new expressway that led to Caracas. Somewhere off to the left where darkness had begun to obscure the mountains was the old road that Jeff had once traveled with his heart in his throat because of the precipitous grades and hairpin turns. The thought of it made him grateful for the new highway, not only because of its safety but because it cut the traveling time in half.

For the sense of urgency was still riding him. Even though he was more than twelve hours late he had the feeling that time was important, that even a half-hour saved might make the difference between success and failure. He tried not to think about Karen Holmes and the trick she had played on him in Miami, and he refused to consider the possibility that she might already have accomplished her purpose.

Once he had talked to Harry Baker he would know where he stood and what must be done as the next step. He had cabled Baker of his delay before he left Miami. He felt certain Baker would be waiting at the hotel, and as his brain continued to speculate he was only vaguely conscious of the broad divided highway, the viaducts that bridged the valleys, the mile-long tunnel that bored directly toward the city.

They were on the outskirts now, and the lights that blanketed the valleys and hillsides reminded him of Southern California and the sprawling growth he had seen on the way back from Korea. A broad avenue he did not even remember cut directly through the downtown part of the city, and then the cab had turned left and was winding along paved drives that always sloped upward until a final turn brought them into the semicircle that fronted the hotel.

A porter moved across the flagged terrace and down the walk to meet him, and by that time the driver had opened the trunk to remove the bags.

"*Gracias*," Jeff said. "*¿Cuánto vale?*"

"*Treinticinco* B's. *Treinticinco* bolivars."

Jeff shook his head. "No B's," he said. "Dollars. U.S."

A man coming along the walk, apparently from one of

the long row of parked cars, assessed the situation and stopped, a lean, dark man with an aquiline nose and a sharp-featured face. Now he addressed the driver in Spanish and when the reply came, turned to Jeff.

"He says ten dollars will be satisfactory."

Jeff thanked him, paid the driver, and then he was following the porter up the walk and into the lobby which opened laterally in front of him. The desk was on his left and he gave the clerk his name and said he had a reservation, noting as he did so that the clock on the back wall pointed to 8.08.

He filled out a registration form and was asked for his passport. The clerk listened as he explained why he did not have a passport. He took the tourist card and birth certificate, saying that they would be returned later, and now Jeff asked if Harry Baker was still at the hotel.

"In 312," the clerk said. "I have given you 314."

When he had changed a twenty-dollar bill into Venezuelan bolivars Jeff followed the porter toward the elevators. Looking through a glass partition at the rear he saw rows of tables set up in what looked like a private dining-room, the men milling about with drinks in their hands. He asked the elevator operator about it and after a moment of concentration the boy's face brightened.

"PanAm Oil Company," he said. "Once each month they have this business dinner."

314 proved to be a single room, one side of which was a tall three-paneled window. The porter hung up Jeff's coat, put the largest bag on the rack, and checked the carafe to see that it was full. He accepted Jeff's two-bolivar piece with a *Salud*, bowed out, and then Jeff stepped to the windows, finding two of the panels fixed and immovable while the third opened inward and was guarded by a screen.

Outside the screen was a narrow balcony with double rails and Jeff unlatched the screen door and stepped out.

From there he could look down on the swimming pool with
its underwater illumination and the lights that had been
strung across the terrace adjoining the bar. But because
he was still obsessed with the thought that time was so
important, Jeff gave his attention to the windows of the
adjoining room. When he saw the cracks of light behind
the drawn curtains he knew what he wanted to do.

Not bothering to wash or unpack, he picked up the room
key, stepped into the hall and knocked at the door on his
right. With the light on it never occurred to him that Harry
Baker would not be there, and when he had knocked once
more he tried the knob and the door swung inward.

He took a step, hearing the door click shut behind him.
The overhead light was on but the room seemed empty
and he said: "Harry?" tentatively as he took his second
step. That was when he saw the figure on the floor partly
obscured by the foot of the bed.

For another second surprise and shock held him motion-
less, his gaze fixed on the hips and legs and upturned
shoes. Then he was moving, round the foot of the bed,
stepping over the legs to kneel beside the torso, knowing
now that this was Harry Baker.

Once more he said: "Harry!" His voice tight.

He saw the telephone on the floor near the outstretched
hand, the overturned ashtray which had been knocked
from the desk. He shook a limp shoulder and reached for
a hand that was as warm as his own. Then, even as he
tried to find a pulse-beat, he saw the moist dark stain on
one side of the white shirt.

The coat of the tan, lightweight suit was open and he
saw the tiny hole on the right side, the black smudge en-
circling it. His fingers were damp and trembling as they
dug into the limp wrist, and he tried again with his other
hand before he understood that there was no pulse here,
that Harry Baker was dead.

3

JEFF LANE was never sure how long he stayed there on one knee beside the still figure. Time no longer seemed important and his mind was stunned and there was only the sickness churning at the pit of his stomach.

Very gently he released the wrist. He found his handkerchief and dried the palms of his hands and gradually, as his brain began to function, his thoughts revolved not about the reason for Baker's death but about the man himself.

For he had liked Harry Baker. He had not known him well, but he had talked with him a half-dozen times since he had been working on the case, had had drinks with him twice. He remembered that Baker had been in G-2 in the Army, that he had worked as a police officer in California and as a security man for one of the Las Vegas luxury hotels before coming east to accept this job with the Boston office of a national agency. Nothing that he had known about Baker indicated that he was anything but a shrewd and capable detective, and an honest one.

In this present assignment there had been no reason for violence. Baker had been looking for a man and he had found him. He had even cabled that his job was done and—

Jeff's thoughts hung there as he recalled the other words of that cable. A temporary job was to keep Baker in Caracas. What sort of job? For whom? Why—if that was the reason—had this job led to murder?

When Jeff understood there could be no immediate answer to such questions he glanced at the telephone and knew he would have to use it. He started to turn his head, still on one knee. That was how the shadow of some movement caught the corner of his eye, and what he did then could be attributed to the lingering traces of shock and nerves too tightly tuned. With no certainty that he had seen anything at all, he was suddenly breathing shallowly while an odd coldness spread across the back of his neck.

Turning only his head, he looked behind him at the curtained windows, one of which stood open and only partly covered. The bottom edge of that curtain stirred gently in the night breeze. Certain there was nothing here, he continued his inspection, his dark gaze prying as it swept the room and came to rest on the small entrance hall.

The door to the bathroom stood open and there was only darkness beyond. Opposite, another door, to the closet, stood ajar, and it was from this direction he had thought something moved. Slowly then, making no sound, he came to his feet, not knowing what he was going to do, only knowing that he had to be sure. On tiptoe he moved across the rug. When he saw the bathroom was empty, he wheeled and yanked at the closet door.

All this was done impulsively, without thought of the consequences. Under the circumstances it was a foolhardy attempt that could easily have been dangerous or even fatal, but not until then did he realize his mistake and consider the odds.

For he had known that Harry Baker had been shot and there had been no gun in sight. Now he understood why. He seemed to see it first, even as the faint odor of perfume mingled with the air of the hallway.

The backward step he took was instinctive as he stared at Karen Holmes, no longer dressed in her smart sharkskin suit and dark-red hat but wearing a summery navy-blue frock which was topped by a white-flannel jacket. In her left hand she clutched a blue bag; in her right hand was a short-barreled revolver.

Jeff let his breath out slowly, while the girl stood there tensed and immobile, her young face white with shock. He found the back of his throat dry and swallowed. He took another small step backward and this brought him up against the edge of the bathroom door.

"Well," he said as casually as he could. "Come on out."

"I—I didn't know who it was," she said finally, her voice small.

Jeff waited, giving her time but not wanting to retreat any farther. He saw her body relax. Presently she took a tiny step and then another and now, with the light on her face, he could see that the dark-blue eyes were wide open and rimmed with fear.

The gun wavered in her hand. He could see the muzzle wobble as it dipped downward. Then, as though its weight was too much for her to support, her hand sagged and now Jeff grabbed for it, holding the muzzle down and then twisting the gun from her unresisting grasp.

He took a new breath as he moved back into the room, but there was a tremor in his hand as he flipped out the cylinder and examined the six shells, one of which bore the neat little indentation of the hammer.

"One shot, hunh?" he said.

He hesitated and the resentment that had been working on him all day merged with the reaction of the moment so that his voice was flat and accusing.

"Maybe I was lucky," he said.

"What?"

"You only gave me a mickey."

He heard her gasp as her mouth opened. "But—" She swallowed and tried again, a desperate cadence in her voice. "You don't think—"

"Don't I?"

"But it's not my gun. I've never had a gun. It was on the floor."

"Sure."

"But it was, I tell you."

"What were you doing here in the first place?"

"We were going to have dinner."

"Oh?" Jeff said, still edgy. "You work fast."

"But I knew him before. In Boston. My father knew him." She swallowed again and now the words came tumbling out. "We were going to have a drink first and I waited on the terrace and he didn't come and it was cooler than I thought so I came up to get this jacket." She touched the white coat. "My room is down the hall so when I came past I thought he might still be here. I knocked and the door was unlocked and I saw the light on." She ran out of breath and when she continued her energy was spent.

"He was on the floor just like that. I didn't know what the matter was until I saw the blood and the gun. I don't know why I picked it up; I didn't even know that I did. Then I heard the knock—

"I was scared, don't you understand?" she cried, her voice shaking. "I was petrified. I—I didn't know what to do or who might be coming and when I saw the closet—"

She let the sentence dangle, as though she had run out of explanations. She watched Jeff put the gun on the desk behind him and then he stepped up and took the bag from her hand. What she had said, the way she had said it, had sounded convincing. But he could not forget how convincing she had been on the flight down from New York and this time he intended to be sure.

When he had the bag open, he glanced at the handkerchief, tissues, compact, lipstick, cigarettes and matches, the change purse. But it was the leather folder that interested him and when he took it out and opened it he looked incredulously at the photostatic copy of a document that proclaimed that Miss Karen Holmes of such and such an address had been licensed by the State of Massachusetts as a private detective.

"A private detective?" he said in his bewilderment.

He peered at her, his brow furrowed and dark eyes brooding.

"A private detective?"

He saw the spots of color tinge her cheeks. Slowly her chin came up and now her eyes were bright and defiant.

"What's wrong with that?" she demanded.

"And you're working for Tyler-Texas."

"I work for the Acme Agency."

"All right, so Acme is working for Tyler-Texas. Who supplied the knockout drops, or did you brew them yourself?"

For an instant then she faltered. "I—I had to do that."

"Sure," Jeff said with heavy sarcasm. "I guess it's written in your contract."

He waited for her reply because he thought she was going to make one. He saw her lips part and then something happened. While her eyes blinked to keep back unwanted tears her mouth suddenly tightened and her rounded chin set stubbornly. That look was enough to remind him that it was childish to work off his resentment at a time like this. He did not believe she had shot Harry Baker and what had happened yesterday no longer seemed important. He returned her bag and stooped to pick up the telephone.

It was a dial phone and when he had the hotel operator he told her to send the manager to room 312 and to call the police.

The manager arrived first, but the two uniformed policemen from a radio car were not far behind, and since they spoke nothing but Spanish there was little Jeff could do but stand beside Karen Holmes and listen.

After the first outburst one of the officers went to the telephone and dialed. He spoke rapidly for ten seconds and hung up. His partner bent over the body and experimented with the limp hand and wrist and carefully replaced it. By now the man at the telephone had seen the revolver, but he did not touch it. He stood with his back to it, his partner joined him, and they waited silently, eyes fixed on Jeff and the girl, grim-faced but very neat in their khaki uniforms with the Sam Browne belts and crisscrossed straps and heavy holstered guns at their hips.

The manager, whose name was Andrews, was a chubby, florid-faced man with thin colorless hair and an apoplectic manner. It was clear that he blamed Jeff and/or Karen Holmes for what had happened and his tone of voice suggested he would sue them both for defamation of the hotel's reputation at the earliest possible moment.

"You say you found him?" he said. "Which one of you?"

"Both of us," Jeff said.

"But how? Why should you be here in this room at all? When did you check in, Mr. Lane?"

Jeff told him, and then because he was tired of Andrews he said: "Look. When the detectives get here—if that's what they have in Caracas, and assuming that one of them can speak English—we'll tell what we know but there's no point in telling it twice. If you want to wait you can listen in."

Andrews sputtered and had a little trouble with his breath but he did not suffer long because the door opened a few seconds later and two men came in, one of them big and young looking, the other one older and thinner. At the sight of the big man the two uniformed men stiffened to attention while he spoke briefly to them. They replied and one pointed to the gun. When they had touched their caps, they detoured along the wall and left the room.

The big man took off his light-gray felt and put it on the

bed. He had a light-complexioned, strong-boned face and black eyes that had a hooded look beneath the heavy brows. The eyes were busy in the few seconds as they inspected the dead man without moving closer and then considered Jeff, the girl, and finally Andrews.

When he was ready he spoke to Andrews. There was a brief exchange while the florid face grew more so. Finally Andrews shrugged and left the room. When the door closed the man turned back to Jeff.

"I told Mr. Andrews that we would send for him when we needed him," he said, with only a trace of accent. "I am Ramon Zumeta, chief of our Homicide Section."

"Jeffrey Lane," Jeff said. "This is Miss Karen Holmes."

"And this one?" Zumeta glanced toward the floor.

"His name was Harry Baker," Jeff said. "A private detective from the States."

"Ah—you knew him?"

"He was working for me."

Zumeta nodded and spoke in Spanish to his companion, who had been emptying Baker's pockets and now stopped to pick up a small straight-backed chair and carry it to the far side of the bed by the window. When he motioned the girl to sit down she thanked him and Zumeta said:

"Who found him?"

"I did," Karen said, and repeated the story she had told Jeff but with somewhat more detail.

"And you, Mr. Lane?"

Jeff started with his arrival at the airport and told what he knew. There was no interruption. Zumeta would nod from time to time but only the intense steadiness of his gaze suggested that he had filed, catalogued and cross-indexed everything he had heard. Now he went over to the desk and looked at the revolver.

"You found this on the floor, Miss Holmes. You picked it up without thinking and took it into the closet? And you took it away from her, Mr. Lane?" He shrugged and picked it up. "Then if there were any worth-while finger-prints on it—which is doubtful—there are none now."

He gave the weapon a quick inspection and put it into his coat pocket; then turned as someone knocked at the door. His assistant opened it and a man came in with a doctor's bag, followed by two men with a rolled-up stretcher.

The doctor said: "*Hola*, Ramon," and went immedi-ately to the body. He applied his stethoscope, pulled out the shirt, and checked the small bluish hole in the chest, making an occasional comment as he worked and point-ing now to the blackish smudge on the coat front. When he spoke to the men with the stretcher, Jeff turned to face the window, pulling the curtain back from the open sec-tion. Karen Holmes was already looking out into the night and he stood above her, seeing the lighted pool and ter-race, the winding street beyond the hotel grounds that curved upward into the near-by hills. He stood that way, trying not to think, but conscious of the hardness in his throat, until he heard the door close.

Almost immediately there was another knock and as he glanced round he saw Zumeta talking to three plainclothes-men in the hall. When they went away Zumeta came back to resume his questioning.

"Perhaps you could tell me in what way Mr. Baker was working for you?"

"He had been trying to locate my stepbrother."

"His name, please."

"He was known here as Arnold Grayson."

"Ah—yes. I know of him. And was that not his right name?"

"That was the name he was born with. When his mother married my father he took the name of Lane."

"And how long had he been missing?"

"I hadn't seen him in four years."

"What made it important that you find him?"

"My father died two months ago," Jeff said. "He left some shares in our company to Arnold provided he could be located and came back to claim them within three months. I promised to find him if I could."

He took Baker's cable from his pocket and waited for Zumeta to read it. Zumeta returned it and considered the girl.

"You were to have drinks and dinner with Mr. Baker," he said. "You knew him well?"

"Well—no. I'd met him in Boston and my father knew him."

"But you're not here just as a tourist."

Karen hesitated, but not for long. "No, I came to see Arnold Grayson too." She opened her bag and produced the leather folder and for once Zumeta registered surprise.

"This I did not know," he said softly. "Policewomen I have heard of in your country, but private detectives—"

He left the thought unfinished and Karen said: "My agency represents a company that would like to buy the shares that Arnold Grayson would control—if he returned. I came to make him an offer."

Zumeta seemed a bit puzzled, his tone of voice said so. "But Mr. Baker did not work for you. How then did you know Mr. Grayson was in Caracas?"

The question made her glance at Jeff. She hesitated, as though giving him a chance to tell his side of the story. When he remained silent she lowered her glance.

"My office didn't tell me how they knew," she said woodenly. "They only told me where I could find him and that I was to make him this offer."

"You knew about this, Mr. Lane?"

"Not until today," Jeff said.

"I see," Zumeta said in a tone that suggested quite the

opposite. He frowned and bunched his lips. "You arrived at Maiquetia this morning, Miss Holmes. Did you see Mr. Grayson?"

"Late this morning."

"Did he accept your offer?"

"He—he said he would let me know."

The statement was like a reprieve to Jeff. He had foreseen the question and had been afraid to speculate on the answer. Unconsciously he had held his breath while a cord tightened across his chest and now the tension was gone and he could breathe again. She had picked him up; she had tricked him, and got in the first word, but he still had a chance. He was in no mood to gloat but he felt immeasurably better as Zumeta said:

"And you have not seen Mr. Grayson since?"

"Oh, yes. I saw him this evening."

"Oh?" Zumeta bent his head slightly. "When was this?"

"About seven thirty."

"Be so good as to tell me about this."

"I was in the writing-room addressing postcards," she said. "Mr. Baker was with me. I had already said I would have dinner with him and we agreed to meet at eight for a drink."

"Yes," Zumeta said with some impatience.

"Well, from those windows you can see the front terrace and the walk and I saw Mr. Grayson coming toward the entrance. Mr. Baker saw him too."

"What happened then?"

"Mr. Baker said: 'Ah, there's my man,' and looked at his watch."

"Have you any idea what Mr. Baker meant by this?"

"No, I haven't. He just said he'd see me at eight and went away. I suppose he went to meet Mr. Grayson, but I can't be positive."

Zumeta paced two steps, turned, and came back. He

glanced through the contents of Baker's pockets which now were spread out on the desk.

"How long did you remain in the writing-room?" he asked and immediately held up his hand to forestall a reply as a new thought came to him. "Tell me everything you did after that, and at what time."

"I came to my room and showered and touched up my nails. When I finished dressing I started downstairs. That was about eight, or a minute after."

"You heard nothing when you passed this room?"

"No—" She stopped, eyes widening. "Yes, I did too. I heard the phone ring as I came past. It was still ringing when I turned the corner and I thought that meant Mr. Baker was in the bar. That's why I was surprised when I glanced in and didn't see him."

"You did not sit in the bar?"

"No. I was alone and—well, I thought I'd wait on the terrace."

"Yes. And you found it chilly and came to get your coat. When would that be?"

"I'm not sure. I guess maybe five or six minutes after eight. Maybe more."

As she finished, Jeff wondered how accurate her estimate was. He recalled that it was eight minutes after eight when he had stopped at the downstairs desk. He had been there two or three minutes at the most. He had not seen her on the front terrace, but he realized also that there was more than one terrace. Before he could pursue the thought someone banged on the door. When the assistant opened it a voice called: "Ramon!" and then a thin, untidy individual pushed his way into the room and grinned at Zumeta.

"Ah," said Zumeta. "The *Bulletin* is quick tonight."

"Not quick," the man said, in accents that were unmistakably American. "Just lucky. I'm downstairs covering the monthly dinner PanAm Oil puts on and I see some of your boys nosing around. So I do some snooping on my own. Who got killed?"

"An American private detective called Harry Baker."

"What?" The man peered at Zumeta and his Adam's apple bobbed up and down. "Harry Baker?"

"You knew him?"

"Sure. He came to the *Bulletin* when he hit town because we're the only English-language daily and he didn't speak much Spanish."

IIe had been watching Jeff and the girl as he spoke and now he came round the bed and offered his hand.

"I'm Dan Spencer," he said. "Are you Jeffrey Lane?"

"Yes," Jeff said and shook the bony hand.

"Harry said you were coming," Spencer said, his eyes curious as they watched the girl.

Jeff introduced them and Spencer said: "How do you do, Miss Holmes. . . . Look, I don't know what this is all about but if you can—"

"You will find out," Zumeta cut in. "Soon we will go to *Segurnal.*"

"Me too—I hope," Spencer said.

"You, too. But for now, sit down and be quiet."

Spencer sat on the edge of the bed next to Jeff and began to pack a straight-stemmed briar. At close range he seemed to be in his middle thirties, a round-shouldered man with the sort of ingrown stoop that gave his chest a concave look. His skin was sallow; his hair was mouse-colored, shaggy, and carelessly combed. His lightweight suit was baggy and he wore a sport shirt open at the collar, disclosing the upper fringes of chest hair that extended nearly to the hollow in his throat and added to the general impression of untidiness. For all of that he had a friendly, engaging manner, and when he had his pipe going he took out a folded sheaf of copy paper and a pencil.

"What can you tell me?" he said.

"Not much," Jeff said. "Miss Holmes had a date with him and stopped in to see if he was ready. She found him on the floor."

He stopped as the door opened and one of Zumeta's men came in to report. After that there was a small parade of goings and comings, but as each exchange was in Spanish Jeff understood none of the information. Apparently Spencer did, for he made a note from time to time and so did Zumeta. The only break in this routine occurred when Zumeta went into the closet and began to search the two suits that hung there.

When he came out he had a pigskin wallet in his hand. He said something to the man who had given him the information—whatever it was—and then looked through the wallet, counting the bills, taking out what looked like two cablegrams and reading them, checking the papers in the pockets. When a man came in with a fingerprint kit Zumeta moved round the bed.

"We will go now to *Segurnal*," he announced. "Mr. Grayson will join us there."

4

THE HEADQUARTERS of *Segurnal*—short for *Seguridad Nacional* and sometimes known as the secret police—was a modern stone building which occupied a corner on avenida México. Zumeta lead the way into the lobby, past a clerk and the information desk and up the steps into a large air-conditioned room that was surrounded by smaller rooms and separated from them by glass partitions.

A half-dozen men in plain clothes lounged in the center room talking and reading magazines as Zumeta led his procession past them and along a corridor; then down several stairs to another lobby which gave on a side entrance that was now closed, barred, and further secured by a locked chain. The party came to a halt here while another clerk telephoned ahead and a dark man in a baggy suit and a shapeless felt hat stood near by and eyed them silently. At a word from the clerk, Zumeta continued up the stairs to the second floor and across the corridor to a recessed anteroom, open at the front but railed in.

Here the telephone procedure was repeated and presently they all filed through the gate and into a windowless air-conditioned waiting-room with paneled walls and leather-upholstered furniture. Zumeta stopped and waved them to seats.

"You will wait here, please," he said and went on through the next door.

Jeff sat down on the divan next to Karen. He was impressed; he said so to Spencer.

"Somebody's got a lot of protection."

"Maybe he needs it," Spencer said.

"Who?"

"Pedro Vidal. He's the head man here. All over for that matter; it's a national organization." He grunted softly. "You should feel honored. He's a hard man to see."

He sat down to relight his pipe and Jeff brought out cigarettes and offered them to Karen. She hesitated, but finally took one, murmuring her thanks and leaning forward for a light. Her face was still pale, but composed now, her body relaxed, the dark-blue eyes resigned and withdrawn. When she leaned back there was something so appealing about her that Jeff considered offering some words of reassurance. Then the moment passed and his thoughts moved on. He glanced at Spencer, wondering if he could answer a question that had been bothering him ever since he found Baker. He spoke of the cable.

"Baker said he had a new job," he said. "Would you know what it was?"

"All I know is that he went to Barbados on Saturday and came back yesterday morning," Spencer said. "Why, I don't know." He shook his head. "It's a rough deal," he said. "He was a good guy. I used to know him in Vegas when I was working for a paper out there. If a thing wasn't legit he wouldn't touch it. That's why I can't figure this one."

He stretched his legs and sucked idly on his pipe, frowning, the side of his thumb scratching the hairy triangle at the base of his throat. After that the silence came until Jeff thought of something else and put it into words.

"Maybe you knew my stepbrother in Las Vegas. Arnold Lane."

"Lane?" Spencer glanced up. "Sure. At least I knew who he was. He's in town here now—I guess maybe you knew that—except he calls himself Grayson." He might have said more if the outer door had not opened at that moment to admit the man they were talking about.

In that first instant when Arnold Grayson made a quick inspection of the room Jeff started to rise. It was an automatic impulse based on the social habit of shaking hands with someone you had not seen in a long time. Then he knew that such a gesture would be sheer hypocrisy, just as he knew that Grayson would probably ignore it.

"Hello, Junior," Grayson said, all the old arrogance Jeff remembered so well still in his voice. "I hear your old man finally decided to cut me in on the family fortune. What happened? Conscience bother him?"

Jeff settled back, a muscle bulging in his jaw as his mouth flattened, his eyes dark with resentment but his temper in hand as he was reminded of the job he had to do. He had come a long way and he realized it would be foolish to antagonize his stepbrother at this point. He sat still, noting the changes the last four years had made.

Taller than Jeff, more muscular in his younger days, Arnold Grayson was still well proportioned, the excess weight skillfully minimized by the well-cut double-breasted suit. The face was puffy but tanned, the wavy light-brown hair was thin and sharply receding, and a small mustache—a new addition—helped disguise a too-small mouth that, Jeff knew, could be smiling and twisted with fury in alternate minutes. For all of that he had about him a look of importance when viewed objectively; only those who knew him understood how impressed he was with his own self-importance. Now Jeff gave him a small mirthless smile.

"Sit down, Arny," he said casually. "Relax."

But Grayson was not yet ready to sit down. "Hello, Miss Holmes," he said. "Hi, Spence. What's this about Harry Baker?"

"Somebody shot him," Spencer said.

"Where?"

"They didn't tell me."

"I mean, where was he?" Grayson said, his impatience showing.

"In his room. Miss Holmes had a date for dinner and stopped by to see if he was ready." Spencer waved his pipe. "He was on the floor."

"When was this?"

"Who knows?"

Grayson looked at Jeff, vertical grooves at the bridge of his nose and worried glints in his light-gray eyes. The change in his manner was at once apparent to Jeff and he wondered why this should be. Before he could speculate, the inner door opened and a swart, white-haired man with the features of an Indian beckoned.

They filed past him, Spencer leading the way, and continued across a second windowless office. Its only other occupant was an attractive young woman who sat behind a flat-topped desk and watched them pass through the door on her left. This opened into a third paneled office, larger than the others but still without windows.

Zumeta stood beside the desk. Behind it and also on his feet was Pedro Vidal, who was as tall as Zumeta but leaner, an immaculately groomed man with well-kept hands and thick black hair. He bowed slightly as he acknowledged Zumeta's introductions. When he asked them to sit down his voice was quiet, his English excellent.

Apparently Zumeta had briefed him well because he turned at once to Jeff and said: "I understand you employed Mr. Baker to find your brother—"

"Stepbrother," Jeff cut in.

"—to inform him of a recent inheritance," Vidal went on, ignoring the interruption. "How long since you had seen each other?"

"About four years."

Vidal glanced from one to the other. "You have a dislike for each other? There is some bad feeling?"

"What?" Grayson said.

"You have not seen each other for four years yet when you meet—or had you met earlier this evening without telling Zumeta?—you do not even bother to shake hands."

"How the hell do you know?" Grayson said.

Vidal showed no annoyance at the remark, but swiveled his chair and pressed a button. With that a square of what had looked like black glass recessed in the wall behind the desk was brightly illuminated and Jeff found himself looking at a miniature view of the waiting-room as seen from above.

"What's that, television?" Grayson asked.

"Mirrors," Vidal said as the light vanished. "A sort of

periscope." He allowed himself a small smile. "It is sometimes wise to know exactly who wishes to see me."

"And hear what they say, hunh?" Grayson added.

"When advisable." Vidal leaned his forearms on the desk.
"You understand now why I asked the question."

Jeff cleared his throat. "No bad feeling," he said. "Just
nothing much in common. Arnold's seven years older
and—"

"Just say we're not buddies," Grayson said. "We never
were. Jeff doesn't approve of me; neither did his father."

Vidal considered the information.

"Yet he made provision for you in his will. . . . Tell me,
Mr. Lane," he said. "What would happen if you had not
located your stepbrother—or if something happened to
him?"

"My sister and I would have received Arnold's share,"
Jeff said.

"I see. Now about this evening"—he glanced at Zumeta
—"we have a timetable that should be helpful but before
we go into that I would like to say that we have checked
the gun, which apparently killed Mr. Baker, with his permit. It was his gun. This suggests—though there could be
other answers—that whoever came to his room came with a
gun and relieved Mr. Baker of his gun. Later, when it
became necessary to shoot—Mr. Baker might have made
the mistake of resisting—Baker's gun was used."

He paused and took time to examine each face in turn.
Before he could add to the statement, Grayson spoke.

"That's very interesting, but what I'd like to know is
why I was brought here in the first place."

"Because," said Vidal, "you may have been the last one
to see Mr. Baker alive."

Grayson leaned forward, his pale eyes hostile. "Who says
so?"

"Miss Holmes," Zumeta said, and went on to relate her

ONE MINUTE PAST EIGHT

story of Grayson's meeting with Baker. The corroboration that followed came unexpectedly from Dan Spencer.

"She's right about that," he said.

"Oh?" Vidal's black brows climbed. "How do you know?"

"I was there, in the lobby." Spencer took the pipe from his mouth. He explained his assignment to cover the monthly dinner and said: "They were to have a guest speaker over from the States and I tried to get a line on him from the dinner committee. I thought if I could button-hole him and get a copy of his speech I could duck the dinner part. . . . I saw Grayson come in and speak to Baker. They went over toward the elevators."

"And you?" Vidal said.

"When they told me the speaker might not get there until around eight fifteen I went into the bar."

A faint buzz on the desk punctuated the sentence and Vidal picked up one of the four telephones from a shelf behind him. A moment later he covered the mouthpiece and frowned at Grayson.

"You sent for Luis Miranda. . . . Why?"

Spencer, sitting next to Jeff, leaned over and spoke from the corner of his mouth: "A lawyer. A good one."

Grayson gestured emptily. "I didn't know why you sent for me," he said. "I hate to get caught out alone. I got picked up for speeding a while back and they held me over-night in jail and fined me three hundred B's."

"That is the usual procedure on a first offense." Vidal smiled. "It is a good way to cut down the accident rate. . . . But that was the city police, not us."

"Also," Grayson said, "you've got a law here that says you can hold a man for thirty days without a hearing."

"True," Vidal said. "Thirty days, at which time you are brought before a judge and it is decided whether I can hold you longer without preferring charges. But I should remind you that if I think I have cause to hold you for thirty days, an attorney would do you little good. Neither would your consul or your ambassador. However—" He spoke into the telephone and hung up.

The man who entered a moment later was straight-backed and distinguished. His dark suit had a silken sheen, his hair was touched with gray, and his swart, sharp-featured face was impassive as he glanced about the room. In that same instant a muted bell rang deep down in Jeff's consciousness. For it seemed to him that somehow Luis Miranda seemed familiar, though he could not remember why.

He puzzled over the thought while the lawyer greeted Vidal and Grayson. There followed a long exchange in Spanish and then Miranda leaned back while Ramon Zumeta took over.

"We have questioned some of the help at the Tucan," he said, "and have established certain facts. You came to the hotel about seven thirty, Mr. Grayson. Mr. Baker met you. Do you care to tell us what you did then?"

"Why not." Grayson slumped in his chair and now he smoothed his hair with the palm of his hand. "I went up to his room, stayed about one minute, and came down. I went home. You can check with the servants."

"At approximately ten minutes of eight," Zumeta continued, "Mr. Baker came to the desk to ask if there were any messages. He went from there to the bar and ordered a dry martini. When it was served he reached into his pocket and then told the barman he must have left his wallet in his room. The barman remembers this because he told Mr. Baker he could sign the check, but Mr. Baker said he would rather pay and to hold his drink. He never came back for it."

Zumeta glanced up, hesitated, then consulted his notes. "At about five minutes of eight Mr. Baker came to the desk to ask for his key. The clerk could not find the regular key, so he offered a duplicate, thinking Mr. Baker had left the other one in his room. He saw Mr. Baker start for the elevators, but he cannot remember whether he saw Mr. Baker actually step in or not."

He glanced at the girl. "You were right about the telephone call you heard. At 8.01 someone used a house phone and the operator rang room 312 three times before the party hung up. At 8.07 the light on 312 flashed on the switchboard. When the operator answered someone said: 'Outside,' and was given a line. She thinks it was no more than fifteen or twenty seconds before the telephone was replaced. Unfortunately, because of the dial system, we do not know where the call went. Unless he died instantly, which is doubtful, Mr. Baker could have pulled the telephone to the floor and made that call. . . . Would you know anything about that call, Mr. Grayson?" he asked.

"Me? No. I'd just talked to him a half-hour before that."

"About what?" Vidal asked.

"A personal matter." Grayson sat up, the grooves digging into the sides of his nose and his pale gaze intent. "What did you find in the room?"

"Aside from the usual things, the gun," Zumeta said. "His traveling bag was unlocked and the keys were in the lock."

"But— I mean, wasn't there anything else?"

"Clothing, Mr. Grayson. His wallet, the usual papers. . . . Should there be something else?"

Grayson's glance slid to Luis Miranda and he jerked it back. He cleared his throat and shrugged. "I wouldn't know," he said. "I just wondered if you found some clue, something that would give you a lead."

Under the circumstances the reply lacked conviction and Jeff wondered about this when Grayson slumped in his chair and the scowl deepened. Then Zumeta said:

"Is there anything any of you can add to the information we have?"

On the other side of him Karen Holmes sat up. "I don't know if it's important," she said, "but Mr. Miranda was at the hotel too. He came in right after Mr. Grayson. I remember seeing him from the writing-room windows."

It was then that Jeff remembered. For he was certain now that this was the man who had served as an interpreter for him with the taxi driver. *But that was later,* he thought. Not when Karen saw him.

"This was about seven thirty, Miss Holmes?" Vidal glanced at Miranda as she nodded.

"Quite true," Miranda said, his accents precise. "I am one of the attorneys for PanAm Oil, as you know. I was included in the guest list for tonight's dinner. In fact," he added, "I was paged there by my home. That is how I knew Mr. Grayson wished me to come here."

"Did you see Mr. Grayson at the hotel?" Vidal asked.

"Not that I recall."

"Or Mr. Baker?"

"No."

"Mr. Spencer"—Vidal fixed his gaze on the reporter—"you say you went into the bar after you saw Mr. Grayson and Mr. Baker. How long did you stay?"

"Quite a while. I was still there when I got the idea something was wrong."

"Did you see Mr. Baker?"

"Not after the first time."

"But—"

Spencer grunted and dug absently at the base of his throat. "I wasn't in *that* bar, Chief. I'm a reporter. I can't afford to pay four B's for a Scotch and soda very often. Not when there's a Company bar set up in the private dining-room."

Miranda stood up and spoke in Spanish to Vidal. Presently he nodded and turned to Grayson.

"There seems to be no need for me here at this time," he said stiffly. "Mr. Vidal has assured me that no one will be detained tonight and I have other business to attend to."

"Wait a minute!" Grayson jumped up, his eyes flaring and his voice mean.

"You will excuse me," Miranda said as though he had not heard.

"But you can't walk out on me without—"

He stopped as the door slammed in his face, his neck red with anger and his mouth twisted. As he stood there Jeff eyed him with some amazement because, though it was obvious there was ill-feeling between Grayson and the lawyer, he could not understand the reason for the outburst. Then, the fury still riding him, Grayson wheeled on Vidal.

"How much longer does this go on?" he demanded savagely.

Vidal eyed him narrowly but his voice remained calm.

"Not long," he said. "One more question. Our records show that Mr. Baker went to Barbados on Saturday and returned yesterday morning. It has been said that you engaged his services."

"So what?"

"I wonder if you would mind telling us the nature of his work and why he went to Barbados."

"Sure I mind," Grayson said. "Not because it's important but because I don't think it's any of your business."

Vidal shrugged and his mouth tightened as he reached for two sheets of paper on his desk. When he separated them Jeff could see they were cablegrams.

"These were found in Baker's wallet," he said. "I will read them to you." He gave the date of the first one and said: "This was addressed to Mr. Harry Baker, Marine Hotel, Barbados and says: 'Accept offer. No reprisal on Lane if cash. Advise immediately where and when delivery will be made.' It is signed 'Westwind,' and was sent from Las Vegas, Nevada."

He glanced up. "I am curious about the reference to the name *Lane*." He fixed his dark gaze on Jeff. "Would this be you?"

Jeff shook his head. When he said he had never been in Las Vegas Vidal considered Grayson a silent moment. "And you, Mr. Grayson, used to be known in the States as Arnold Lane, is that true?"

"What about it?"

Vidal hesitated, then picked up the second cable. "This is to the same name and address. It reads: 'Carl Webb will make collection Wednesday.'"

He put the message aside and glanced at Spencer. "You once worked in Las Vegas. What is the Westwind?"

"A hotel."

"Do you have any idea about these cables?"

"Not the faintest."

Once more Vidal considered Grayson. "It seems obvious you sent Baker to Barbados to make some offer in your behalf. Perhaps you can tell us who Carl Webb is."

"I never heard of him before."

"And you do not wish to tell us what this offer was about."

"Not now I don't."

Vidal turned his hand palm down on the desk. "As you wish," he said. "But we will require a statement from you in the morning, Mr. Grayson. Ramon"—he glanced up at Zumeta—"will be in touch with you. . . . *Buenas noches, señor.*"

He turned to Karen when Grayson left. "If you are ready, Miss Holmes, one of my men will drive you to your hotel."

He pressed a button and spoke to the man who appeared in the doorway.

"What about me?" Spencer said. "I'd like to get this story in. How much of this can I tell?"

"The facts of the murder, Mr. Spencer. The circumstances but no suspicions. You can say the police have several leads and the matter is being investigated."

He picked up the telephone, though Jeff had heard no buzz, listened, and said: "*Si.*"

"You can ride with Miss Holmes," he said to Spencer. "You will find the car at the main entrance— Oh, Mr. Lane," he added. "Just a minute more, if you please."

Jeff waited in front of the desk and Vidal leaned back in his chair. "As I understand it, Miss Holmes is competing with you for the shares your stepbrother has recently inherited. If this is so, I can understand why you were here, since Mr. Baker was working for you. What I can't understand is how Miss Holmes knew your stepbrother was here."

"Neither can I," Jeff said.

Vidal frowned. "You are from the same city in the States? You knew her there?"

"I never saw her before"—Jeff hesitated, his tone ironic as certain memories came flooding back—"until I met her on the plane coming down."

"Then perhaps you would give me your opinion. From what you know would you say Miss Holmes had any reason to kill Mr. Baker?"

"No."

"You believe her story?"

Jeff knew what his answer would be, but he took a moment to think back and erase all prejudice. When he spoke, his grin was fixed.

"If you mean about what happened tonight, yes."

"Thank you." Vidal rose. "We like Americans here. Your

businessmen have done much for this country and it is bad
publicity when one of you is murdered. We shall do our
best to find out who is responsible. . . . We will need
your statement in the morning. You do not speak Spanish?
Then Ramon can handle it."

"Where did you learn English?" Jeff said as his curiosity
got the best of him.

"In the States mostly. Ramon and I have spent some
time in Washington. In your F.B.I. school."

5

THE MAN in the baggy suit and shapeless felt Jeff Lane
had seen at the foot of the stairs was waiting outside the
gate of the second-floor anteroom. With a gesture that ordered Jeff to follow, he led him downstairs and back
through the main room to the front entrance. Not until
they were on the outer steps did he stop and wave one
hand to indicate Jeff was now on his own.

There was still a lot of traffic on the Avenue but up beyond the trees which lined it the sky was clear and bright
and the air was dry and comfortably cool. Not knowing
exactly where he was, Jeff turned left toward a lighted
shop on the opposite corner, hesitating on the curb to light
a cigarette, and at the same time watching for a cruising
taxi. He did not know he had company until he heard the
voice beside him.

"Señor Lane?"

Jeff flipped the match away and turned to find the man
at his elbow. Slender and not very tall, he was clad in a

dark suit, and Jeff studied him a moment, trying to penetrate the shadows that obscured the face while he wondered if this was a touch of some kind. Curious as to how the fellow knew his name, he let the silence build. The sentence that followed got his undivided attention.

"I have heard what happened to Señor Baker."

"How did you know who I was?"

"I have friends in *Segurnal*. I have been waiting for you."

"Why?"

"Señor Baker has told me about you. I have done some work for him. I was outside the Tucan tonight when you arrived, though I did not know who you were then, nor did I know what happened until much later."

Other questions came to Jeff's mind but it suddenly occurred to him that this man, whoever he was, might prove very helpful indeed. That he seemed to be offering his services seemed clear, and when Jeff understood this he touched the man's elbow and said:

"Let's get a beer and talk some more."

"I would like that," the man said and kept pace with Jeff as they crossed the street and entered the corner store which had a cigar-stand in the front and a restaurant in the rear. They found a table along the wall and gave their order, and now Jeff could see that the man was neatly dressed, that his hands were clean, that his eyes were bright and alert. He was getting bald on top, which made it difficult to guess his age, but when he smiled he looked younger than Jeff had first thought.

"I am Julio Cordovez," he said simply and seemed pleased when Jeff offered his hand. "My work is the same as Señor Baker's. He came to me because he did not know the city or our language. He needed help."

"Did he get it?"

"He seemed satisfied with my work."

"And you think I might need some help too, is that it?"

"I thought I should speak to you."

Jeff grunted softly. "Well, you could be right, Julio. How much do you charge?"

Cordovez tipped one hand, his tone apologetic. "As you know things are expensive in this city. I was paid eighty B's a day for my services and the use of my car. I thought now I should offer you my services if you so desire."

"At the same price?"

"No. For my expenses only. I do not know why anyone should kill Señor Baker. I liked him. He was a good friend. If I can help find out who did this thing I will be only too happy. But it is difficult to work alone. It presents problems, and those in *Segurnal* will want to know who I represent."

Jeff grinned at him, liking the little man and his forthright answers. "What you mean," he said, "is that you'd like a client."

"It would be easier for me."

"O. K.," Jeff said. "You've got one. The same pay."

"It is not necessary but"—Cordovez shrugged and his smile came—"if you insist I will be most grateful."

Jeff did not say so, but he had an idea he was the one who should be grateful. He knew no more about the city and the language than Baker had known, and he needed help; a lot of help. He sampled the beer the waiter brought and spoke of the two cables the police had found in Baker's wallet. He asked if Cordovez knew Baker had gone to Barbados for Grayson.

"Oh, yes."

"But you don't know why?"

"Baker told me he was going, but he used an expression I did not understand. I was not sure what he meant. He said he had a chance to make a quick 'score' for a few days' work. Would that mean a lot of money?"

"Something like that."

"And I know this. Baker knew Grayson in the States. In a place called Las Vegas, but under another name. From things that were said I think Grayson could not go back until he had settled some accounts. It was for this he needed Baker's help. I think he was frightened about something."

Jeff nodded, remembering how Grayson had looted the treasury of the partnership his father had established and wondering if something of that nature had happened in Las Vegas. When he finished his beer without speaking, Cordovez asked if there was anything he could do for Jeff tonight.

"I'd like to take another look at Baker's room," he said, "if you think you can get in."

Cordovez said he thought he could, and this proved to be no idle boast. For when they walked down the third-floor hall of the Tucan, fifteen minutes later, he had a ring of keys in his hand and it took him only three tries to turn the lock.

Jeff moved in first to snap on the light, and Cordovez stopped to turn the bolt. "Strangers do not always understand such locks," he said. "They assume the door is locked when they leave but this is not so. It is necessary to use a key from the outside."

"Oh," Jeff said, understanding now how Karen Holmes had been able to walk in to find Baker dead, how he himself had walked in on her.

"You think the police may have overlooked something?" Cordovez said.

"Probably not," Jeff said, "but there's no harm in trying."

He glanced round, aware that the window was open, the curtain bulging with the night breeze. He stepped to the chest and began to open drawers and then, at some small sound behind him, he stopped.

"Easy!"

It was a voice he had never heard before, and as he turned he saw Cordovez standing very still, his gaze fixed on the man who apparently had slipped from behind the curtain, a compactly built fellow with a wide, thin-lipped mouth and a muscular jaw. His face was deeply tanned, his curly light-brown hair was cut short. He was well dressed and at first glance looked like a successful young business executive, which, in a sense, he was. What spoiled the illusion was the gun in his hand.

"Where's Harry Baker?" he said.

Jeff felt some of the tension slip away, and with his surprise in hand a feeling of resentment began to smolder inside him.

"Dead," he said.

The man's eyes opened and anger flared in their depths. "Don't kid me, chum!"

Jeff jerked his head toward the desk. "There's the phone. Call the secret police and see. . . . Go ahead, we'll wait."

Something in Jeff's tone lent weight to his words and he saw the doubt build in the man's face as his glance shifted to Cordovez and back again.

"When?" he said.

"Tonight," Jeff said, and then he went on, his phrases curt and succinct as he explained what had happened. When he talked that way he was convincing, and the doubt he had first seen in the man's face expanded into concern and perhaps consternation. The gun dipped as he moved forward.

"And who are you?" he said finally.

Jeff answered that one too.

"Arnold Lane's stepbrother?" the man said, his frown deepening.

"He didn't use that name here," Jeff said.

"Don't move, señor!"

The words had a flat and dangerous sound. Jeff knew they came from Cordovez but he did not know why until he turned his head. He had seen no movement, nor, apparently, had the stranger. But there was a gun in the little detective's hand now, a big gun. It was pointed properly and his bright narrow gaze was a little frightening.

"Don't move!" he said again. "Especially the gun."

The stranger never had a chance and he seemed to know it. He froze where he was, his own gun still tipped toward the floor. He waited that way while Cordovez slid round behind him, reached down, and relieved him of the snub-nosed revolver. Moving backward now, but not once shifting his gaze, he flipped out the cylinder and tipped the shells on the desk. When he had put the gun beside it, he replaced his own.

"This, I think, is better," he said. "To see a gun in the hands of a stranger always makes me nervous," he said. "Now we can talk. Your name, please, señor?"

"Carl Webb," the man said and let his breath out in an audible sigh. "From Vegas. I had a date with Baker but the plane was two hours late leaving Panama."

"Sit down," Cordovez said. "Let us discuss this date you speak of."

Webb sat down. So did Jeff. Cordovez, his arms folded, leaned against the desk. Webb glanced from one to the other.

"You followed the investigation tonight?" he asked. "Was there any money found here?"

"Not that I know of," Jeff said.

Webb took a breath and reached into an inside pocket. He brought out what proved to be four cables, two which he had received and two which were copies of replies that he had sent. He handed them to Jeff, who glanced through them quickly to see if they were arranged by dates. He noticed that the two copies were the same messages that Pedro Vidal had read at *Segurnal* and now he said:

"You work for the Westwind Hotel? Doing what?"

"I'm one of the assistant managers."

"You knew my stepbrother when he was out there?"

"He worked for us," Webb said, the corner of his mouth dipping as though he found the recollection distasteful. "We knew him plenty. Baker, too. He was one of our cops for a couple of years."

Jeff gave his attention to the first cable, which had been sent from Barbados on Saturday. It read:

Offer 120 thousand to clean up Arnold Lane matter. If acceptable and no reprisal cable Harry Baker, Marine Hotel, Barbados, B.W.I.

The amount mentioned startled him but he went on to read again the message found on Baker which spoke of the acceptance of the offer.

The third cable, addressed to the Westwind read:

Cash ready for collection your convenience room 312 Tucan Hotel, Caracas, Venezuela. Advise.

The fourth message was the one saying that Carl Webb would collect this evening.

Jeff returned them. "What's the rest of it?" he asked. "Did Arnold run out with a hundred and twenty thousand?"

"One hundred grand, even," Webb said. "Nearly three years ago."

"How could he get his hands on that much?"

"Because in our business we deal in cash." Webb pulled out a silver case and stuck a cigarette into his mouth. "We have to. You never know when some guy—and some are pretty big operators—is going to get hot and hit you for plenty."

He got a light and said: "Arnold Lane went to work for us about four years ago. He was a big, good-looking guy with plenty of personality when he kept it turned on. He dressed the place up and he was smart. They gave him more and more responsibility and finally let him handle the take and the payroll. One day about a year later he took off with a dame who had just gotten her divorce. We traced them to Los Angeles and lost them."

"You sent a couple of your boys to Boston," Jeff said. "We sure did."

Cordovez cleared his throat. "You would have had Grayson arrested and sent to prison?" he asked.

"Grayson?" Webb paused, a faint smile touching his mouth. "So that's the name he uses here. . . . No," he said to Cordovez. "It's not that simple. In the gambling business you deal in cash. You have to have people around you that you can trust and you have to keep them honest because there's a lot of temptation. We get a few chiselers, a stickman who's a thief, things like that, but when a guy scoops a bundle it's no good going to the cops."

He pointed his cigarette. "Take Lane—or Grayson. He takes us for a hundred big ones and suppose the cops finally catch up with him. O. K. He gets a lawyer and maybe gets off with a couple of years. So suppose he's spent most of the boodle? Where do we get off? Un-unh," he said and his mouth twisted.

"We handle things like that ourselves. A guy turns out to be a heavy thief he has to pay the hard way. It's always been done that way and that's why it seldom happens any more. We have to make an example, you know what I mean?"

"I think so." Cordovez nodded. "You dispose of this man who has robbed you."

"Right," Webb said. "And we make sure the word gets around. Maybe we still take a loss, but we make a point.

It keeps the rest of the help straight all over town, because they know the same thing can happen to them. It's very simple. I don't know all the answers, but I can figure part of this. Grayson wanted to come home and he knew that if he did he'd eventually wind up at the side of the road with a couple of slugs in his head. He was ready to pay off, with a bonus, but he was still running scared. He didn't know if we'd accept his offer and he was afraid to handle it alone. He was even afraid we'd find out he was in Caracas. So he hired Baker to front for him and sent him to Barbados as a decoy."

He put out his cigarette. "Well, it happens we're ready to deal. We take the dough and spread the word that Grayson found out he couldn't beat our system and paid off with a bonus to save his neck. In this country the deal works out because they don't care how much money you take out. No smuggling. Just pack the cash in a bag and take off. They don't care in the States either and it doesn't have to be dollars. We'd even accept payment in bolivars because it's a real hard currency."

He hesitated and then stood up and by that time the rest of the picture was crystal clear in Jeff's mind. Apparently his stepbrother had done reasonably well since coming to Caracas, but he'd had no intention of returning—until Baker had located him and word had come of his inheritance. To claim it he had to return to Boston, and because the gain there was greater, he had raised the cash. He had made his deal through Baker, and it seemed obvious that he must have brought the cash here to this room tonight.

"It's a good motive for murder," he said, half to himself. "The first one we've had."

"What?" Webb said.

"Cash. A lot of cash."

"Somebody beat me to it, hunh?" Webb's grin was tight

and mirthless as he stepped over to the desk and picked up his gun and the shells. As he started to load them Cordovez stopped him.

"Please," he said politely. "Not until you leave, señor."

Webb understood the suggestion. He tucked the revolver inside his jacket and pocketed the shells. "You're pretty handy with one of these, Julio."

"Thank you." Cordovez made a small bow. "I have had much practice. For many years I was an assistant chief with *Segurnal.* . . . And what will you do now?"

"Sleep on it, I guess," Webb said. "I came a hell of a long ways to make a collection and I'm not going back empty-handed if I can help it. I think Baker had the dough ready for me. Somebody took it."

He stopped at the door and turned the bolt. "I'm going to start looking, Julio. I think our friend Grayson had better start looking, too. Because he's still in hock. He knows it and I know it. . . . See you," he said and went out.

Cordovez buttoned his jacket. "A very determined young man," he said. "And possibly a dangerous one. Do you agree?"

Jeff said he agreed and smiled to himself at the little detective's phrasing. He looked round the room and suddenly he had no further desire to search it. He was tired, depressed, and discouraged. And in the morning, or sometime soon, he would have to face his stepbrother, a thought which served only to heighten his discontent.

"All right, Julio," he said. "Let's forget it for tonight. Can you be here in the morning?"

"I will be here on the front terrace when you come down for your breakfast." He made his customary bow. "*Buenas noches,*" he said and started along the hall.

Jeff watched him make the turn into the corridor leading to the elevators before he got out his key. He unlocked his door and then stopped as something caught his eye on the floor. He knew then that a note had been thrust under the door and stepped back into the lighted hall to read it. It was very short and had no salutation:

Please stop at 320 when you get in no matter how late. K. H.

6

KAREN HOLMES wore a pastel-gray flannel robe that was securely belted and buttoned at the neck. Ballet-type slippers cut her height down so that the robe trailed slightly, and when Jeff followed her into the room he saw that her face had a pink, scrubbed look and the corners of her eyes were sleepy.

"Thank you for coming," she said. "I didn't know how long you would be so I curled up here." She indicated the easy-chair in the corner. "I must have fallen asleep."

She asked him to sit down and he swung out the desk chair, waiting until she had settled down on the one she had just left. While she made sure her knees were covered he had a chance to see that her hair had been combed out and fell softly along the sides of her face, and it occurred to him that she was more attractive this way than she had been on the plane. But he had not forgotten the Miami incident and waited with a mounting curiosity to see what she had to say.

"I had to talk to you," she said finally. "I—I wanted you to understand."

She hesitated, looking right at him now. When he made

no reply she folded her hands and put them on one knee.

"I'm not apologizing for coming here," she said. "I was hired to see if I could get an assignment of the stock your stepbrother will inherit. I still intend to try."

"Then what is there to explain?" Jeff said. "You picked me up and steered me into the restaurant and gave me a mickey. You had a job to do and you did it. It didn't matter how you did it or what means you used. I suppose if I'd refused the drink your pals there in the airport would have slugged me."

"That's what they said. That's why I had to use that powder."

"Oh," Jeff said. "Then you didn't make it yourself?"

That one brought the color to her cheeks. Her back seemed to stiffen and the dark-blue eyes had sparks in them.

"All right," she said spiritedly. "If you don't want to know the truth perhaps you'd better go. I can assure you it's no fun for me either."

He eyed her steadily for a long moment and decided she meant what she said. He also knew, though he could not tell why, that it was important to hear what she had to say.

"I don't blame you for being angry," she said. "If it will help any to know I'm ashamed of myself, I am. But if—"

She let the sentence trail. A small sigh escaped her. She no longer looked like the smart and worldly secretary she had claimed to be on the flight to Miami. With her head slightly bowed and her glance averted, she looked so feminine and desirable that his defenses were weakened and some of his annoyance evaporated.

"All right," he said. "Let's start over. You work for the Acme Agency. Let's start there."

"I'm afraid I'll have to start before that. It will take a while and it won't be easy." She sighed again and her glance came up. Then, as though determined to make the effort, she straightened her shoulders. "I suppose you wonder why I'm a private detective."

"Frankly, yes. I bought that insurance secretary routine. That I could believe."

"What I told you about Wellesley and the secretarial school was right," she said, "but that was not what I wanted when I was growing up. My father is a retired police captain. I had a brother who would have been a policeman too if he hadn't been killed in the Pacific in 1945. I've read about little boys who want to grow up to be cowboys or baseball players or engineers. Well, I wanted to be a policeman."

She tucked one foot under her and said: "At first my father accepted the idea because he thought I would outgrow it. Then, when we heard about my brother, Edward —I was twelve then—it seemed even more important. I couldn't be a policeman, but I could be a policewoman. There was never any doubt in my mind. I took Dad's kidding—he still wouldn't believe I was serious—and I went to college as we'd planned. It wasn't until I graduated that we really had it out together.

"He said I should go to secretarial school. He used every possible argument against my being a policewoman and when he realized I was still determined he thought of a compromise. He's the one who suggested I try being a private detective. He had some friends in the business and there were times when a woman was useful. If I would go to secretarial school he'd give me one year as a private detective without interference; he was willing to gamble that one year would cure me of the idea."

She looked up without moving her head. "I guess it sounds childish now," she said softly. "I guess it is childish. But when you grow up with an idea that seems so important it's not always easy to put it aside. With me I suppose it was a minor obsession." She sighed and said:

"So I did some studying and maybe Dad pulled some strings. Anyway I got the license and went to work and it couldn't have been more dull. Sometimes I would follow people. I was never told why. I simply followed them—or tried to—until my feet were sore and my legs ached. When the day was over I wrote a report and that was that. I worked behind department-store counters, all kinds of counters, spying on the help to make sure they were honest. I felt like a spy. I hated it. I never had an exciting moment in nine months or even a very interesting one. Then they told me about coming here."

"How did they know I was coming?" Jeff asked. "How did they know about my stepbrother?"

"They said there was a leak in your office."

"When did they tell you?"

"Saturday."

"That was a quick leak," Jeff said dryly. "This was the Tyler-Texas outfit that found this out?"

"Yes. Actually I don't know the details. All I know is that my boss said he had a job I'd like. He knew what plane you were taking and we tried to get a reservation on an earlier flight but by the time I managed to get tourist cards from the consul there wasn't any earlier flight. It wasn't until I got to the airport and you were pointed out to me that I even knew who you were."

"They told you to pick me up."

"Yes. They said the only chance I'd have to get the assignment from your stepbrother would be to get to Caracas first. All I had to do was get to know you and make you invite me to have a drink in the terminal restaurant. I asked why and they said the less I knew the better. They said they had been in touch with their Miami correspondents and that someone would meet me and take over. That's why I had to wear the red hat and the gardenias; so the men would know me."

"What exactly were you supposed to do?"

She straightened her leg and leaned forward, elbows on knees, her voice hardly more than a whisper.

"They told me that when I got into the building I was to excuse myself and say I was going to the rest-room. Two men were to meet me and tell me what to do." She wet her lips and said: "It scared me a little. I wanted to know what the men were going to do to you and they said not to worry, that there'd be no trouble. They had a way to make you miss the plane and I'd go on alone. . . . Well, I didn't know what to say. They made it sound so exciting and—" She groped for a word and Jeff supplied it.

"Romantic?"

"I suppose so," she said and blushed. "And there was another reason. I was the one who wanted to be the private detective. I wanted to do something that was exciting—I'd been pestering them for a long time—and I couldn't go to Dad and say I was afraid. I just couldn't. My—my pride wouldn't let me."

Jeff understood that much and it moved him strangely to know that while pride made her take the assignment, pride did not prevent her from letting him know how she felt.

"So these two men met you," he said.

"Yes. And one of them gave me this little folded paper. He said to send you to the cigarette machine and put the powder in your drink. He said you'd never taste it. It wouldn't hurt you, and when you started to get drowsy I was to bring you outside and they would handle the rest of it."

Again the color touched her cheeks and again her voice grew small. "I told them I couldn't. I knew then that they must have planned the whole thing before I left Boston. And now they said I had to do it. They weren't even polite about it. They said: 'Either you'll do it, sister, or your friend will get hurt. We were hired to do a job and we intend to do it one way or another.'"

She hesitated, her eyes wide open, as though each detail was imprinted on her brain.

"They meant it," she said.

"They probably did," Jeff said.

"They said if I did what I was told they'd get you in a cab and take you to a hotel and let you sleep it off. If not, they'd handle it their own way. . . . I had to," she said a little desperately. "I was afraid not to. I don't expect you to forgive me, but I do hope you'll believe me. Somehow it seems terribly important."

Jeff stood up and found his neck was stiff. He twisted it, all resentment gone now and moved deeply by this girl and the things she had said.

"I believe you," he said, hesitating as he looked down at her and wanting very much to speak some word of reassurance. When no such word came to mind he smiled at her and said: "Maybe, under the circumstances, the mickey was better than a broken skull. Thanks for telling me about it."

He stopped at the door and turned back. "But you're still going to try to get that assignment."

"Oh, I have to," she said, as though there had never been any question about that particular point. "I have to try."

He grinned at her as he went out. He said he was sorry he couldn't wish her luck, but he at least understood the quality of the competition.

He found that he was humming as he moved along the hall, but he did not know there was a grin on his face that was supported by some inner glow that seemed warm and satisfying. He unlocked his door and turned on the light. He snapped the bolt behind him and then stopped short when he saw his two bags, knowing instinctively that some-one had transposed them on the luggage rack.

They were not locked—he had not bothered after clearing customs—and when he opened them he could tell that they had been searched. When he straightened his mouth was grim and there were somber glints in his eyes. There was nothing in the bags of great value and nothing was missing. But the fact that someone had been interested enough to risk a search reminded him that he was in the middle of an ugly situation he did not entirely understand.

7

JULIO CORDOVEZ was waiting on a bench just outside the main entrance when Jeff came downstairs the following morning. He looked very neat in his tan suit; his white shirt was freshly laundered, his shoes were polished, and the bald spot on his head was pink and shiny. He made his customary small bow and his smile was broad as he offered his greeting.

"You slept well?" he asked.

"Very well," Jeff said, which was true. "How about some breakfast?"

"I have finished mine."

"Coffee?"

"I would like that very much."

They crossed the lobby and went along the hall past the private dining-room to a long high-ceilinged room bright with morning sunlight. The captain gave them a table by the windows, and as Jeff sat down he had his first look at the city, which sprawled below him in the distance, a heterogeneous panorama of structures that followed the valleys and crept up hillsides brown from lack of rain. Near the center tall buildings spoke of rapid growth and here and there modern, boxlike structures indicated a growing interest in low- and middle-class housing projects.

Jeff spoke of the view and mentioned his earlier trip, remarking at the change. Cordovez nodded. "It is only just begun," he said. "They cannot build fast enough and everywhere you see businessmen—from the States and England and Germany and Italy."

He fell silent as Jeff worked on his bacon and eggs, sipping his coffee and pulling on a cigarette that gave off a pungent aroma. As Jeff poured more coffee, he said: "You have plans for this morning?"

"Do you know where my stepbrother lives?"

"In the Valle Arriba district."

"Is it far?"

"Perhaps twenty minutes."

"I'd better call him first."

"I have written the numbers for you." Cordovez brought out a slip of paper and pointed. "This is the residence; this the office."

The voice that answered Jeff's call to Grayson's home was female and Spanish. He had sense enough to try the word *señor*. When this got him nowhere he tried *señora*, and presently another woman answered, her accent clipped and polite.

"Oh, yes," she said when Jeff identified himself. "Arnold said you were coming. . . . I'm sorry he's not here just now. He left for his office about ten minutes ago. Do you have the number?"

Jeff thanked her and dialed again. This time the woman who answered had some command of English but no better news. The best she could do was offer the information that Grayson had phoned to say he would not be in until later.

Jeff relayed the information to Cordovez as they went outside, and the little detective offered a suggestion.

"Perhaps it could be Señor Webb."

"What?"

"If your stepbrother has not paid his debt, he could be worried about Señor Webb."

"I guess he could be at that," Jeff said; then, as a new thought came to him: "Do you know Luis Miranda?"

"The *abogado?* Oh, yes."

"What do you know about him?"

"A very old family," Cordovez said. "At one time they had much land but they were not always on the right side —how do you say it?—politically—and there is less now. But still much. An estate in the Guarica River district near Calabozo, a beach house at Macuto, a fine home in the Country Club section."

"Would you say Luis is wealthy?"

"I would say so."

"Wealthy enough not to be tempted by one hundred and twenty thousand in cash?"

"It is a lot of money; but"—Cordovez shrugged—"I do not think Luis would steal just for money."

"Married?"

"Twice. The two children are grown. The son manages the estate and the daughter is in the States. His second wife is a countrywoman of yours. Very beautiful."

"Do you know where his office is?"

"Of course."

"Then let's go."

He followed Cordovez out to a three-year-old Ford which had been parked along the semicircular drive, and presently they were rolling down a quiet, tree-lined street, turning right at the end to make the descent into the city. Here the newness of the houses, the modernity of the architecture that had been built into the many small apartments impressed Jeff greatly, but he noticed that every ground-floor window was protected by an ornamental metal grill.

He mentioned it. He asked if they were necessary.

"Oh, sure," Cordovez said, and laughed. "At night there are always prowlers. It is best to be safe."

The traffic thickened as they came into the valley and there were times when it stalled completely. Yet no one seemed greatly disturbed and not once did a horn blow. He mentioned this, too, and Cordovez said:

"To do so means jail or a fine. It is against the law."

"But don't things get awfully jammed up?"

"Oh, yes. And when it becomes unbearable we do this to show our displeasure." He put his arm out the window and began to pound the heel of his hand against the side of the door. "Near the center in the late afternoon it sometimes sounds like thunder," he said, and laughed again.

The building that housed Miranda's office was square, tall, modern, and, because of the stunted appearance of its neighbors and its distance from the center of the city, strangely incongruous. Cordovez double-parked in front of it and asked if he should wait. Jeff thought it over and said no.

"I don't know how long I'll be and if you've got friends at *Segurnal* why don't you snoop around and find out what they know."

"Very well." Cordovez tore a sheet out of a small note-book and wrote down two numbers. "My home," he said; "my office. I am in touch every hour. Someone will take your message."

Luis Miranda had a suite on the fourteenth floor, and when Jeff walked into the paneled, air-conditioned ante-room he remembered the airport building and *Segurnal* and decided that whoever had the air-conditioning agency in Caracas was doing all right. The pretty brunette at the desk took his name and picked up a telephone. When she hung up she said:

"Mr. Miranda will see you in a few minutes."

Jeff walked over to the window and looked across the valley at a hillside that was crawling with bulldozers and trucks. Dust rose like brown fog to be carried away by the morning breeze and the scars that showed so clearly spoke of another development in the growth of the city.

He was still there when the light tap of heels behind him caused him to turn in time to see a striking-looking blonde in a figured-cotton dress bearing down on him from the direction of the inner corridor. She had an erect, full-breasted figure that was big-boned and ripely rounded; she also had the height to complement the curves. Her hair, worn rather long, was straw-colored, and her face was broad across the cheekbones and richly tanned. Her eyes, which looked as if they had been rinsed in bluing earlier that morning, were bold but friendly in their appraisal and contrasted sharply with the tan that spread smoothly down the deep V of her dress.

"Hello," she said. "You're Jeffrey Lane, aren't you?"

"Why—yes," Jeff said, deciding that the hair was natural and putting her age somewhere around his own.

"I'm Mrs. Miranda," she said. "Arnold's told us quite a lot about you."

"Oh?"

"I'd like to talk to you if you have the time. . . . I'll wait for you in the car," she said—as though everything had been decided. "A blue Buick just across the street and very badly parked." She smiled. "You can't miss it."

The little brunette watched her go. When she caught Jeff's eye she pointed to the corridor. "The last door," she said.

Luis Miranda's office was as impressive as the man himself. A corner room, it was darkly paneled except for the wall of books, and the furniture was heavy-looking and expensive. Miranda stood until Jeff was seated, smiled, and folded his brown, long-fingered hands, exposing a star sapphire in what looked like a platinum mounting.

"What can I do for you, Mr. Lane?"

"Give me some information," Jeff said, "if you can and if it's ethical."

He lit a cigarette and asked if Miranda knew why he was in Caracas. When the answer was affirmative he went on to explain the situation at the Lane Manufacturing Company and Miranda listened patiently until he finished. Then, to make sure he had the picture, he went over the details in his own way.

"Yours had always been a family business until recently?"

"Yes."

"And what is it you manufacture?"

"Lately most of our business has been in clutches."

"Like on automobiles?"

"Everything but. We have a new principle on a drive that will work on motors of any size. A lot of our clutches go into such things as washing machines, dishwashers, dryers, mixers, power tools. Because of the new drive there is less strain on motors, gears, and bearings, all of which makes maintenance practically non-existent."

"Yes," Miranda said. "So for tax purposes and to clear up your bank loans, you decided to offer stock to the public four years ago. The original one thousand shares held by your family were split two hundred for one, making two hundred thousand shares in all. Your family controlled ninety thousand shares and this, with stockholders favorable to you, was enough to control the company. You do not wish to have this Tyler-Texas Company take over the business."

"They work one of two ways," Jeff said. "They've been buying up shares in the market and if they can get control they'll either take over with an exchange of stock or they'll move in, use up the cash to increase dividends and run the price up, and then unload. If Arnold votes with them," he said, "we're out."

He put his cigarette away and spoke of Karen Holmes. "She saw Arnold yesterday," he said, "and I wondered if he gave any indication to you how he felt or what sort of proposition Miss Holmes made."

"He mentioned something about Miss Holmes offering a bonus."

Jeff thought it over, not liking what he heard, his brows bunching with the effort and his teeth absently worrying his lower lip. When this got him nowhere he decided to speak of Carl Webb and the assignment that had brought him to Caracas.

Again Miranda listened attentively, his expression inscrutable and nothing that resembled surprise showing in his dark eyes.

"What I'd like to know," Jeff said when he finished, "is whether Arnold could raise that much cash. I don't think he'd dare give himself away to Webb unless he did but—"

"He could, and he did." Miranda unfolded his hands and leaned back. He turned one hand over and put it on the arm of his chair and now his voice was mildly sardonic. "Reticence is not one of your stepbrother's qualities. He was and is a very self-possessed man and inclined to be boastful."

His glance moved beyond Jeff to the windows and stayed there. "He lived well since he came to Caracas and supported himself by acting as agent for certain foreign companies. He had some money to invest and made some speculations, not all of them profitable. But he was smart about one thing.

"Two years ago he bought five or six acres in the Valle Arriba section close to the golf club. He put in a street and built a house and subdivided the rest. I understand the house and lot cost him one hundred thousand B's. He could sell now for three hundred thousand."

"Wow!" said Jeff as he figured the exchange at thirty cents American to the bolivar. "Ninety thousand dollars from thirty."

"The remaining half-acre lots he retained, eleven in all. Selling them individually he could get the equivalent of fifteen thousand U.S. dollars each. On Monday he sold the eleven for roughly one hundred and thirty-five thousand— four hundred and fifty thousand B's. I know because I drew up the papers."

"Did he tell you why?"

"He said he was in trouble in the States. Before he could return he would need one hundred and twenty thousand in cash."

"Could he get that cash in dollars?"

"We have a hard currency here," Miranda said, "acceptable everywhere in the world at face value. Anyone can take bolivars to the bank here and receive dollars. But because the bolivar is easily negotiable, there is little call for dollars. It would be difficult to find that many dollars without advance notice. Grayson was satisfied that a payment in bolivars would be accepted for his debt. He needed it by Wednesday. I feel quite certain he had the cash with him yesterday and from what you have told me I must assume that Mr. Baker was to act as his emissary."

"Did you get the idea he intended to return to the States?"

"I feel sure that was his intention." He leaned forward and picked up a stapled report of some kind from his desk, his smile polite but distant. "Does that answer your questions, Mr. Lane?"

Jeff thanked him and stood up, inspecting the sharp aristocratic features of the light-brown face, the smooth-

ness of the gray-streaked hair. Then, prompted by some
impulse he could not analyze, he said:

"How did he get along down here? Was he well liked?"

"Possibly by some. He had great personal charm when
he cared—or found it advantageous—to exert it."

"And you, Mr. Miranda?"

"For myself," Miranda said, "I disliked him intensely. To
me he was, and is, an evil man."

Jeff Lane had no trouble locating the Buick. It was the
same color as Mrs. Miranda's eyes. She used them when he
stopped beside the car, smiling a welcome and inspecting
him frankly. When she stepped on the starter he understood he was to get in and as he slid onto the beige leather
seat she said:

"Where to? I might as well chauffeur you while we're
talking."

"The hotel will do fine," Jeff said.

"The Tucan? Right."

She sat up as she drove and it gave him a chance to study
her profile, the penciled line of her brow, the short upper
lip, the red mouth that suggested a capacity for passion,
petulance, and sulkiness. The deep tan of her face was du-
plicated on the rounded arms that showed beneath the cap-
sleeves and he noticed that her legs were bare and just as
brown. Her voice, though animated, had a faintly husky
inflection as she spoke.

"Arnold told us about his inheritance," she said. "Is it
really true?"

"If he comes back to get it in the next thirty days."

"He said it consisted of stock in your company."

"That's right," said Jeff, beginning to wonder why she
was so interested.

He watched her maneuver into a traffic circle and brake
suddenly when a small truck edged in front of her from

another street. She said something under her breath that sounded distinctly profane and started to bang the horn-ring before she thought better of it.

"Will he be rich?" she asked as she got the car clear of the jam and stepped on the throttle.

Jeff chuckled. "Hardly."

"Oh? But doesn't he get a lot of shares?"

"Quite a lot; but it's not a very big company."

"How many shares?"

"Thirty thousand." Then, because he decided he might as well give it all to her rather than have her drag it out of him, he said: "And right now it's quoted over the counter—or was the last I heard—around fifteen."

She frowned slightly as she did the mental multiplication. "That's four hundred and fifty thousand," she said. "That's quite a lot—I think that's fine," she added, her tone brightening in a way that suggested she was well pleased with the news.

Jeff continued his inspection, noting the emerald engagement ring which must have been four or five carats. When he considered the aquamarine-and-diamond ring on her other hand, and the wristwatch with the diamond-studded bracelet, he wondered why she should be so concerned with money. A further examination of her profile revealed a smile that had taken possession of her mouth. It remained constant as she drove, and the idea came to him that, now that she had the information she wanted, her secret thoughts had been projected well beyond the confines of the car.

"Do you know his wife?" he asked.

"What?" She glanced at him, frowning as her thought-train was shattered. "Oh, yes. Yes, I know her."

"What's she like?"

"Like?" She made a small disparaging sound. "In my

opinion," she said with formidable frankness, "she's a cold potato."

"And how will she like going back to the States?"

In a tone that suggested she could not care less, she said: "I haven't the faintest idea."

She braked the car in front of the hotel and now the smile of contentment had slipped from her face and some inner annoyance was working on her mouth. When Jeff thanked her for the ride she replied indifferently and it was quite clear that his questions had spoiled her morning.

He watched her drive off and then went into the hotel, intending to have another try at locating Grayson; but a man who had been leaning on the desk had another idea. With the clerk acting as interpreter Jeff learned that this was a detective—*oficial* was the word the clerk used—who had been dispatched by Ramon Zumeta to take him to the headquarters of *Segurnal* so Jeff could make a statement.

8

JULIO CORDOVEZ was waiting at the information desk at *Segurnal* when Jeff finished his protracted session with Zumeta and a stenographer. It was then one thirty, and when Cordovez asked if he would like some lunch, Jeff said yes.

"The Normandy is good," the little detective said. "I think they serve lunch. Also, farther in the city there is the Paris. Very old but very good. Or perhaps you would like to see the American Club."

"Is it far?"

"No," said Cordovez and led the way to his car.

He seemed to take a certain pride in showing Jeff the American Club, which had originally been a hotel. He pointed out certain features, showed him the dining-room, the patio, which could be used for special occasions, and the bar, where five American businessmen were shaking poker dice for the third martini.

Jeff ordered an omelet, a salad, and iced coffee, and Cordovez asked for something that turned out to be chicken and rice. He offered no information until Jeff asked for it.

"I have learned the results of the autopsy," he said. "The bullet entered here"—he tapped his lower chest—"and was directed upward toward the back, lodging in the spine."

Jeff sipped his coffee and contemplated his cigarette until the significance of the information struck him. He looked up, eyelids narrowing.

"The spine?" he said thoughtfully. "Then what about that telephone call at seven minutes after eight?"

"Baker did not make it. It cannot be said with certainty that he died instantly, but he would have been paralyzed. He could not have dialed. The doctor does not think he could have lifted the instrument."

"But someone did make a call."

"Yes." Cordovez let the thought build for a silent minute. "You have seen Grayson?" he asked.

"Not yet," Jeff said. "Do you know where he lives?"

"Oh, yes."

"Then let's take a ride. If he's not there maybe I can talk to his wife."

"There is also a man who lives there," Cordovez said as Jeff reached for the check.

"Oh?"

"A Señor Fiske. Dudley Fiske."

"What do you mean, he lives there?"

"He is said to be an old friend of Grayson's and came here a year and a half ago to work as a sort of assistant. Grayson is a man who likes to feel important. I have heard it said that Fiske has many small duties. Also"—he leaned forward and lowered his voice—"he was at the hotel last night with Mrs. Grayson."

Jeff's brown eyes were instantly attentive. "How do you know?"

"I saw them. I have brought Señor Baker to the hotel and have asked if he will need me. He says he is not sure but then he decides it might be well for me to wait. I am parked there where the taxis line up—that is how I notice you, though I do not know who you are—and I see Grayson arrive and then very soon comes this car with Mrs. Grayson driving."

He made a small gesture of apology. "I do not think about this at the time. I do not think about it later. Not until this morning do I wonder why they have come." He started to add to his apology and Jeff cut him off.

"This would be around seven thirty?"

"About that."

"What happened?"

"The woman remained in the car. Fiske started toward the hotel, not by the front, but to the left, around the corner where the grass is and the pool; on the side where your room is. One can also enter the hotel from there."

"How long did he stay?"

Cordovez opened his hands and sighed. "I cannot say. At the time it did not concern me. A few minutes before you arrive they have gone."

"That could be around eight o'clock."

"It is possible."

Jeff let it go at that because he could think of nothing to add. They went back to the car and once under way Cordovez proved to be an informative guide. He seemed to find enjoyment in pointing out the signs of progress in his home city, and Jeff listened absently to the running commentary.

He was told that Los Caobos Park, once a dangerous spot after dark, had been thoroughly cleaned out and was lighted at night. He heard the names of the streets each time Cordovez made a turn. When a modern-looking stadium caught his eye he asked about it and was told that it was the baseball park. A similar structure near by brought forth the information that this was Estadio olimpico.

"For football," Cordovez said and then, pointing a moment to his left, he indicated a new-looking building which stood by itself. "Creole Petroleum," he said. "You have heard of this?"

"Hah," said Jeff with some irony. "I just wish I'd bought a few hundred shares five years ago. Even three years ago."

"This company has brought much money for this country," Cordovez said as he turned into a broad freeway where traffic moved swiftly.

"*Autopista,*" he said. "Avenida de la Mercedes," he added, when he cut right; and then, after another right, they were going uphill, to stop finally in front of an attractively landscaped house that in the States would have fallen into the ranch-type category. "I will wait," he said. "It will be difficult for you to find a taxi here."

A brown-skinned maid took Jeff's name and left him in the entrance hall. The woman who came presently to meet him was slender, poised, and smart-looking, her prematurely gray hair adding to the over-all picture of attractiveness. Her smile seemed automatic as she greeted him and said she was Diana Grayson. She shook hands like a man and led the way into a long, low, cool-looking room that overlooked a wide expanse of well-kept lawn surrounded by a hedge.

She sat down on the divan and took a cigarette from the

silver box on the coffee table, tapping it with nervous stac-
cato movements on the back of her hand before she accepted the light Jeff offered. She inhaled deeply and
crossed her legs.

"Arnold said you might stop," she said. "I'm sorry he's
not here. In fact, I don't know where he is."

"But you know why I came?"

"Oh, yes. He told me that much."

"And do you know if he plans—"

She held up her hand to interrupt him. Her smile was
twisted and her voice was brittle. In its forthright way it
had somehow a savage quality, as though something had
been gnawing inside her until there could no longer be any
need for pretense.

"I think I could save time if I told you I haven't known
what Arnold's plans are or what he's been thinking for
quite a while. I've been married to him for three years and
frankly, Mr. Lane, I'm heartily sick of my bargain."

Jeff blinked at her words and found them embarrassing.
"You—don't get along?"

"That's one way of putting it."

"You married him in Las Vegas."

"As the result of an emotional rebound, I suppose," she
said. "My first husband was a very nice guy, but he was a
drunkard and a weakling. Arnold was never that. I was
completely taken in by his charm, and it was a relief to
have someone who could make decisions and who made
me feel like a woman and not like a nurse. It took me a year
to find out that I had been swindled emotionally and eco-
nomically by that part-time charm."

"But," said Jeff, a little startled by the outburst, "you
stayed with him."

"Oh, yes." She leaned forward and put her cigarette out
by jabbing it forcibly into the metal tray. "Yes, I stayed
with him," she said, her soft laugh a bitter sound. "I could

have gone back to the States if I'd wanted to go empty-handed. I could have got a divorce there but I doubt if you could extradite a man for alimony, could you?

"I had a lump-sum settlement from my first husband. When we came here to make our fortunes I was still in love, or thought I was. Arnold made some investments. He told me all about them when I signed the checks. The trouble was that the bad ones always turned out to be in my name and the good ones in his. Now, except for some jewelry my first husband gave me, I'm practically penniless, and I have no intention of walking out and making it easier for him—not unless I can get a decent settlement."

She did not explain what she meant by making it easier, but her glance moved beyond Jeff and remained there. Then, for the first time, her expression changed and her smile seemed genuinely friendly.

"Come in, Dudley," she said.

Lane turned. When he saw the man who had entered the room he stood up.

"This is Mr. Lane," she said. "Dudley Fiske."

Fiske said: "Hello, Mr. Lane," and offered a chubby hand. A stocky, round-faced man with thinning sandy hair and glasses, he had a quiet, pleasant manner, but Jeff's first impression was that his personality was neutral and that his easy smile came perhaps too easily.

"Sit down, Dudley," the woman said. "Mr. Lane was asking about Arnold's plans," she added as he took a place beside her, "and I was telling him I was afraid I couldn't help."

"Did you know about the money he took from the Westwind Hotel?" Jeff said, deciding he might as well give the question a try.

He watched the smile go away and the mouth tighten again. "Not until a few days ago," she said. "I wish I had. . . . No," she said. "All I knew was that he was in an awful hurry to get out of the country after we were married. I wondered at the time what made him so nervous and jumpy. . . . How much will his inheritance amount to?"

Jeff said he was not sure. It would depend on the price of the stock. "Possibly between four and five hundred thousand."

"Dollars?"

He nodded and said: "I suppose you knew he sold some property the other day."

She glanced at Fiske and then away. "About all he owned," she said thinly, "except for this house."

Jeff hesitated, trying to feel his way along and unable yet to make up his mind about Fiske, who kept watching the woman with an approving smile and something in his eyes that said he was very much sold on what he saw.

"You came down here as Arnold's assistant, Mr. Fiske?" Jeff said.

"That was what I thought," Fiske said, and smiled again. "My trouble," he added with surprising candor, "was that I had a very bad case of adolescent hero-worship and I was a long time outgrowing it. I knew Arnold during his last year in prep school and picked the same college, because he did, though when they kicked him out I stayed put.

"Arnold was everything I wanted to be. Big, good-looking, a fine athlete when he cared to try. He had a handsome allowance and he was willing to share it with someone who could act as his jester and run his errands. At the time I was pretty proud that he chose me because I was in school on a scholarship and I had to work for my spending money. Arnold even took a girl away from me once—it took no great doing—but even that didn't discourage me. He was a great guy and I was his buddy and in my eyes the evil things he did never seemed vicious.

"When he wrote me a year and a half ago I was selling printing in New York and not breaking any records. Arnold drew a fascinating picture about what life was like down here and the amount of money that could be made. He needed an assistant and it was a chance of a lifetime." He raised one hand a few inches and let it fall.

"Apparently I was still enchanted by some of the things that happened a long time ago, or maybe it was just because I was tired of selling printing. Anyway, I came. He moved me right into a wing of my own here. He wanted me in the house because what good is a whipping boy if he's not available? . . . Yes," he said, "I'm an assistant down in the office. I get a salary. Not as much as it should be, but then I get my room and board with the job."

He said other things along the same line, but Jeff heard him only with his ears. His mind had moved to other things and he had an idea that Fiske was telling the truth. He was ashamed of what he had done but not violently so; his bitterness was a passive thing. To Jeff it seemed that essentially this was a nice guy, hard to dislike but with no drive and small ambitions. Such bitterness as he felt had been absorbed with resiliency and he seemed accustomed to shouldering the blame for his failures.

For all this his presence had its effect on Diana Grayson. When she looked at him her brittleness was less apparent and the feminine softness of which she was capable seemed to flourish. Understanding his shortcomings she apparently found in him something that was both comforting and desirable.

"Do you know why Arnold wanted to raise cash, Mrs. Grayson?" Jeff said when Fiske fell silent.

"I'm not sure what you mean."

Jeff told her about Carl Webb and how Harry Baker had been employed to act as the middleman.

"Did you know Arnold went to the Tucan last night with the cash?" he asked.

"Did he?"

"Don't you know? You followed him, didn't you?"

"I beg your pardon."

"You and Mr. Fiske drove up to the Tucan right after Arnold got there." He glanced at Fiske. "You went around the side of the hotel. How long were you there?"

Fiske glanced at the woman as though asking for her assistance and she gave it at once, her voice distant and emphatic.

"I don't know where you got your information," she said, "but this much I can tell you. We didn't follow Arnold and we didn't go to the hotel."

"You knew about the money," Jeff said, persisting. "Luis Miranda knew about it. Who else might know?"

She shrugged thin shoulders and stood up, her glance bleak and her voice astringent. "I'm sorry," she said. "Perhaps you'd better ask Arnold. He may be at the office now."

Jeff rose, aware that the interview was over. He thought he understood a little of the character of these two just as he understood the woman was the stronger. Unhappiness had left scars on her emotions but she had not been broken. That she held her husband in contempt seemed obvious, but to Jeff it also seemed that there remained a calculated desire to make him pay for what he had done to her.

"When Baker's body was found," he said, "there wasn't any cash. I'm pretty sure Arnold delivered it, because he was still scared of the Westwind crowd. Whoever has it now will probably stand trial for murder."

She was looking right at him now, a suggestion of smugness in her smile that was disconcerting. If she was at all worried she did not show it.

"I'd very much like to get my hands on it," she said. "By rights most of it should be mine anyway."

9

ONCE AWAY from the avenida Urdaneta, the broad thoroughfare which had been cut straight through the downtown section of the city from west to east, the streets on the north side were narrow and congested and the buildings were tightly spaced and dark with age and decay. Always there was a slope to the streets and all vehicular traffic moved in one-way patterns. That is why Julio Cordovez, who was to continue on to *Segurnal* in search of additional information, let Jeff out at the corner and pointed to a building a few doors down in the wrong direction.

At this hour of the afternoon the narrow street stood in shadow and to leave room for even a single line of traffic many of the parked cars stood with two wheels on the all too narrow sidewalks. Jeff passed the narrow front of a shop that displayed radios and record-players, an undertaking establishment that featured three open caskets in its plate-glass window, the wider doorway of a garage with a recessed ramp and one gasoline pump and came finally to this entrance, the side of which bore two tarnished brass plates, one of which said: Grayson Enterprises.

Inside there was only darkness and a flight of narrow stairs that led to the second-floor hall. Groping his way along this, Jeff wondered why Grayson should have selected such an address, instead of one of the more modern buildings, until he opened the heavy wooden door and realized that his stepbrother had made himself very comfortable indeed.

For he stood now in a three-room suite, one side of which opened on an inner court, hidden from the street, but green with shrubbery. Thick masonry walls provided natural air-conditioning and no sounds filtered in from outside. A rug covered the ancient tiles of the flooring and the two chairs and the sofa were upholstered in light-green leather. A secretary's typewriter desk stood near a tall window and at the moment Arnold Grayson seemed to be bidding his employee a fond and affectionate farewell.

A cardboard carton beside the desk was half full of discarded papers, and the smartly dressed black-haired girl was holding her bag and a wrapped package as she laughingly protested some suggestion in Spanish. Grayson, in shirtsleeves, had both hands on the girl's shoulders, and even as he glanced at Jeff, he kissed first one cheek and then the other. He turned her toward the door, opened it, and then, as she went past, gave her a resounding smack on a well-rounded hip that brought forth a squeal and a giggle.

But the instant he closed the door his expression changed. Beneath the little mustache the mouth flattened, the tan face twisted, and the pale eyes were arrogant and resentful. His voice was cold, impatient, and accusing.

"What the hell do you want?" he demanded.

The Jekyll-and-Hyde performance came as no surprise to Jeff, but he still wondered if some of the things he had recently read about multiple personalities could apply to his stepbrother. The animosity displayed was of long standing, for he understood that Arnold had always felt that, as the stepson, he had never had the breaks that had been given to Jeff. Now, trying not to show his displeasure, he disciplined his voice.

"You know what I want, Arny."

"Not today," Grayson said, turning on his heel and starting along a short corridor, which led past a smaller office to a larger room very elegantly furnished in a heavy, masculine way. "I'm busy. I've got more important things to do."

Jeff considered the oversized desk, the oversized divan. An open door revealed a small bathroom and in an alcove was a water-cooler, a cellaret, and an icebox. Apparently Grayson conducted his business with all the privacy and comforts of home but at the moment his customary arrogance and assurance were missing. He was tossing papers into an open attaché case on the desk with hands that were fumbling and uncertain. He seemed charged with a nervous tension that was beyond his control. Then, remembering Carl Webb and his mission, Jeff thought he had the answer.

"Did you find the cash?"

Grayson wheeled. "What cash?"

"The cash you took to the Tucan last night."

Grayson's tongue flicked across the lower edge of his mustache.

"What do you know about it?"

"All I know is that someone grabbed it before Baker could make the pay-off." Jeff spoke of his talk with Carl Webb and then he stopped, aware that this was none of his business and that he had a mission of his own to accomplish. "Look, Arny," he said.

"You look." Grayson advanced, his face twisted and the pale eyes bright and threatening. "I told you to get out. I mean it."

Jeff stood his ground. "All I want is your word that you'll vote your stock with us. After all, I didn't have to come here."

"Hah!" Grayson sneered at him. "Don't kid yourself. You've got scruples. You promised your old man you'd try to find me. You wouldn't be able to sleep nights if you didn't try. It's no credit to you, you're just built that way. Now come on, goddammit, get out of here."

He grabbed Jeff's arm as he spoke, wrenched him round

and started propelling him from the room. Jeff took two un-even steps and then braced himself as something that had been building inside him for a long time finally demanded expression. At that moment it seemed to him that all his life he had been pushed around by his stepbrother without once being able to push back, and now, as his temper flared, he took a savage delight in resisting.

It was not his intention to swing on Grayson. He simply wanted to defy him, and now he twisted sideways, freeing his arm as he spun about and pushing his stepbrother away. Apparently Grayson misunderstood the intention, or may-be he just didn't care. Whatever the reason, he attacked at once, and in a fashion that Jeff had never experienced before.

Later he was to wonder where Grayson had learned his tactics, but in that first instant all he knew was that pain exploded in his left leg as Grayson kicked him in the shin, that as he hobbled and started to reach for his leg the right fist came whistling at his jaw.

It caught him a glancing blow at the corner of the mouth as he twisted his head and then he forgot about the pain in his leg. He forgot everything but the overwhelming desire to smash the man who had caused him so much trouble.

It surprised him a little to find how easy it was as he swung his right into the pit of the soft stomach and heard the "whoosh" as Grayson's breath whistled out. He jabbed a left to get the chin up as he came forward. He slugged once with his right, feeling the welcome shock in his hand. Then, as the big man started down, he hooked once more with the right and stepped back.

Grayson dropped on his haunches and put out his hands to keep from toppling over. He shook his head to clear his vision. As the pale eyes focused there was a second or two when surprise was mirrored from their depths, and then the ugliness came, shocking in its intensity.

"Get up!" Jeff said.

Grayson stayed where he was, his face dark with fury and the side of his jaw beginning to swell.

"There's a gun in the desk," he said, his voice checked. "If I get up I'm going to kill you."

Jeff started to reply; he wanted to dare Grayson to try to reach the desk. Then, because he had begun to shake inside, because he realized his own anger could not long be contained, he wheeled and strode from the room.

By the time he reached the street reaction set in. He was breathing heavily and he could feel his knees trembling as a strange weakness seized him. He crossed the pavement and turned to look back at the entrance, no longer aware of his surroundings until he saw someone stop in front of him and heard the familiar voice.

"Hi."

Jeff had to concentrate. He had to steady himself. He had to remember where he was before he could actually see the round-shouldered figure with the hairy triangle in the V of the sport shirt, the shaggy, mouse-colored hair, the pipe that jutted from the sallow face of Dan Spencer.

"I just stepped out for a beer," he said.

"Stepped out?" Jeff said vacantly.

"Sure. The *Bulletin's* just down the street." He took Jeff's arm, turning him so his back was to the street. "How about it?" he asked. "Join me?"

Jeff freed his arm and tried to smile. The one thing he did not want just then was company of any kind. He had to get away, he had to think. He made his excuses as best he could as he began to back downhill.

"No thanks," he said. "Not just now. I—I got a date." He made a pretense of glancing at his watch. "I'm late already."

He knew Spencer was eying him curiously but he could not help it. He could not stand inspection and he turned at once and started blindly down the narrow sidewalk, walking fast until he came to the corner and then slowing down as he approached Urdaneta.

Still not knowing where he was going or what he intended to do, he turned right with the traffic light, walked a block, and then crossed over to his left when the light changed. His steps began to drag. The trembling in his knees stopped and his breathing became regular. The shrill summons of a policeman's whistle at the next corner made him conscious of his wandering and he hesitated while the traffic piled up in front of him.

Not until then did he realize that the corner of his mouth was wet. When he licked it, it tasted salty, and now he took out his handkerchief. There was blood on it when he wiped his lips and he could feel the puffiness at the corner. He began to mutter under his breath as he continued down the street looking for a bar.

He took his first whisky straight and that helped settle his stomach. He poured the second into the iced soda and took his time with it. He was not sure how long because he had begun to think again. When he noticed that two of his knuckles had been scraped each detail of the encounter came back to him. He felt no regrets at what he had done to Grayson, but doubts began to nag him as his mind moved on and he considered the contributing factors.

When he tried to add them up the result was only more confusion. Grayson had not only been worried but very much concerned about something that had nothing to do with his inheritance. Apparently he was expecting someone. Who? Webb? Karen Holmes? Suppose Grayson had in some way located the missing cash? Suppose . . .

Jeff gave up such speculation and finished his drink, convinced now that he had made a mistake in leaving. The smart thing would have been to get out of the office and then wait outside to see who else came to see his stepbrother. If he had had any sense he would have done just that, and now he wondered if there was still time to find out why Grayson had been so upset over his, Jeff's, persistence.

He was not sure how long it had been since he had left the office, and because he still had some small hope of getting back there before it was too late, he walked fast, dodging traffic as he crossed streets and checking the street signs to make sure he made no mistakes. Puffing a little now as he moved uphill he saw the entrance he wanted just ahead and turned in without slowing down. Not until he reached the door at the end of the darkened corridor did he hesitate; then, because he was not sure what might lie beyond, he palmed the knob and turned it silently.

When he had the door open a three-inch crack, he put his ear close and listened. There was no sound but the half-heard thud of his heart. He widened the crack. Still no sound.

On tiptoe now he slipped sideways through the opening and from where he stood he thought he was alone. The outer office still had its empty look, the other doors stood open. Finally, accepting the fact that he was too late, he closed the door behind him and let his body relax. He took a breath and let it out slowly. He glanced out of the high window at the courtyard below and then he started slowly for the room at the rear, having no particular object in mind and no longer thinking about what he was doing.

He was at the doorway before he saw the attaché case on the desk just as it had been when he left. The sight of it left his dark eyes puzzled and he took another step to clear the door. That was when he saw Arnold Grayson.

Three or four feet from the far end of the desk, he was on the floor in almost the same spot Jeff had last seen him. Since that time only two things had changed. Instead of sitting up, the man now lay flat on his back, and the jacket

that had been draped over a chair lay crumpled on the
floor, as though someone had searched it and flung it aside.

Not until he moved swiftly closer did Jeff understand
that there had been still another change: instead of a single
swelling at the side of the jaw, the once tanned face had a
bluish tinge and was ridged with ugly welts.

10

IN THOSE first horrible moments, as Jeff stood there staring wide-eyed at the still figure at his feet, it did not occur
to him that Arnold Grayson was dead. He knew that he
had been savagely beaten about the head with some instrument that left those thin welts. An ear had been torn
and there was blood on the hair above it. The hands, flung
above the head, rested on the floor with the palms up and
he could see that two of the fingernails were stained.

The sight sickened him as he knelt beside his stepbrother and called his name. He reached for the heavy
shoulders and tugged at them. He managed to get the torso
to a sitting position, supporting the dead weight as best he
could. He spoke again, his voice hoarse as he tried to shake
the man awake.

There was no response. The head rolled limply, and now,
the sickness inside him turning coldly to fear, Jeff lowered
the shoulders and put his ear hard against the shirt front.
When he realized finally that the heart-beat he heard was
his own he reached frantically for a wrist and dug his fingers into the warm flesh. He held his breath and tried again.

Only then did he understand that there would never be a pulse.

Somehow Jeff got to his feet and stood a moment, breathing deeply and swallowing hard. Shock and bewilderment made it difficult to think, and all he could do was turn his back and wait until he had his nerves under control. He wiped damp palms on his trousers and flexed his fingers. To occupy himself while he tried to sort out his thoughts, he stepped to the desk, remembering now the gun Grayson had mentioned. He opened one drawer and then another. He tried them all and all were empty. There was no gun; only the attaché case, which was closed but not locked.

He opened it absently, thinking once about the missing cash but realizing it was not here. Papers and envelopes were fastened in small bundles by elastics and when he turned them over he came to the checkbook. It was the sort that has three checks to the page. They had been imprinted with the firm name and now, his mind focusing once more on the money Grayson had raised, he turned to the more recent entries.

The last stub verified the fact that Grayson had indeed found the money he needed. The single word written there read: *Cash.* The rest of the notation was: 400,000 B's—the equivalent of one hundred and twenty thousand dollars. In the deposit column, and dated Monday, was the figure: 450,000 B's, an amount which verified the figure Luis Miranda had mentioned.

As Jeff considered this, his glance moved absently upward to the stub above where a much smaller figure had been written opposite the word—*Airline.*

He spoke the word half aloud, brow puckering as he turned back a page. Here a word caught his eye and he looked again. It was written on the middle stub. *Spence,* is what it said, and the amount was 300 B's.

Jeff turned back two pages to find the identical notation.

When it was repeated again he turned to the front of the book where the first checks in that series had been issued four months earlier. The third stub was marked with the same name and carried the same amount.

He closed the book, replaced it and picked up an envelope which carried the red-and-blue insignia of a well-known airline. He slipped off the elastic and found two tickets dated the following day and giving the flight number and time. The destination was marked as New York. The top ticket was made out in Grayson's name; the second one had been issued to M. Miranda. Then, before he could even begin to wonder about this, the heavy silence was broken by a metallic sound that came from the front room.

Jeff stiffened, every muscle tense, the character of the sound warning him that someone had entered the office. Obeying some impulse that would not be denied, he thrust the tickets into his inside pocket and tipped the top of the attaché case so that it fell shut. When he turned, as ready as he ever would be to face this new threat, he heard the voice call out.

"Hello! Is anybody here?"

In the instant that followed, Jeff's inner tension evaporated and his heart sank. For he recognized that voice and he did not know what to do about it. There was no way out and he could only stand there, feeling the perspiration oozing on his forehead while his scalp grew prickly and a sense of hopelessness blanketed his thoughts. For another second he waited, ears straining as he listened. Then he knew he was trapped.

"Mr. Grayson."

The slow uncertain sound of approaching footsteps continued, and now, because he could delay no longer, he stepped into the doorway.

"Oh!" Karen Holmes said, and stopped. "You."

She was wearing a figured dress with a white background and carrying a white bag. She wore no hat, and though she gave him a tentative smile, her dark-blue eyes remained puzzled.

"I was supposed to see Mr. Grayson at four," she said. "Isn't he—" She stopped, held by something she had seen in Jeff's white-lipped face. "What is it?" she said. "Is something wrong?"

"Yes," Jeff said, and stepped up to prevent her coming into the room. "Maybe you'd better stay out here."

But she had already seen the sprawled figure on the floor and he heard her frightened gasp. One hand fluttered to her breast and she stared round-eyed at Grayson and then at Jeff, the fear and uncertainty she felt reflected in her face.

"Did you—"

"No," Jeff said harshly. "No. He was that way when I came."

"Is he badly hurt?"

"It's worse than that."

"Is he—" Her voice caught and she tried again. "But how— I mean, what—"

"The way it looks," Jeff said, deciding he might as well get it over with, "someone walked in here and beat him to death."

She leaned against the edge of the door, shoulders sagging. Her head sank lower but she said no more, and finally Jeff knew he had to tell what he had done. Because he felt too weak-kneed to stand there any longer he took her arm and gently led her round the desk so she could not see Grayson.

"I only came about five minutes before you did. I didn't know what happened either. I was here earlier and I came back—"

He checked himself because she no longer seemed to be listening. Her gaze was fixed on the hand which rested on the desk, a gaze so intent that he glanced down, seeing first the small dark stain on his shirt front and knowing he must have got it when he held Grayson's torso upright. Then, as his eyes moved on, he saw the back of his hand and the two scars on his knuckles. Already scabs had begun to form there and make them more noticeable than ever.

"Karen!" He reached down to touch her shoulder in an effort to make her look at him. "I told you I was here before. We had an argument and both of us threw a couple of punches. But the only mark he had on him when I left was a lump on his jaw."

And then he was talking fast, a little desperately, beginning from the moment he first walked into the office and relating each detail he could remember. Stopping only to take a breath from time to time, he gave her the complete story because it seemed so important to him that she understand what he had done and accept it as the truth.

She did not interrupt. Her eyes remained on his face and as he continued the doubt that had been there went away. He saw the change in her expression and took heart. When he finished he had the idea that if she did not believe him she at least wanted to believe him.

"That's it," he said wearily. "I just wanted to tell you while I had the chance."

"Chance? What do you mean?"

"I have to call the police, don't I?"

"With the blood on your shirt and those marks on your knuckles? How can you?"

He looked at her, brows screwed up and his eyes peering in his disbelief.

"What else can I do? Run?"

She put her chin out and her mouth grew firm. "How long were you gone?" she demanded.

"I don't know. Maybe a half-hour."

"Did anyone see you?"

"No," Jeff said and then he groaned. "Oh, Lord."

"What is it?"

"Spencer."

"Who?"

"Dan Spencer, the reporter we met last night. His paper is just down the block. I'd just left here and was standing across the street. He was on his way to get a beer. He asked me to join him."

Karen shrugged her trim shoulders and made a face. "Well, there you are. He's certain to remember that. He'll tell the police, and even if he doesn't they'll want to question you. They'll see your hand. How can you explain it? You haven't any alibi, have you? You even have a motive."

"What motive?"

"You'd better think a little more," she said with remarkable lucidity. "You came down to ask your stepbrother to vote his stock with you. Did he agree?"

"No, but—"

"Don't you and your sister get that stock now that he's dead? He had to go to Boston to claim it, didn't he? It couldn't ever be his stock unless he went back. So it's yours now, isn't it?"

For a second or two Jeff could only look at her, a little astounded by the clarity of her thoughts and the way she expressed them. What she had said made sense, and having accepted this much, what finally decided him was the thought of something Pedro Vidal had said the night before in his *Segurnal* office.

This was not the United States. This was Venezuela and the law said a suspect could be held for thirty days without recourse, without a chance of freedom unless Vidal changed his mind. The thought shook Jeff as he considered its ramifications and suddenly he knew he had to take the chance this girl was offering him. What he might prove before he was caught seemed beside the point. He had to try to clear himself and he could not do it in a cell. Julio Cordovez would help and that thought alone was encouraging. Karen would help too if she could. He knew it now as he leaned forward and took both her hands in his.

They were firm but soft and she made no effort to withdraw them; nor did her gaze falter as he looked into her eyes and said what he had to say.

"Thanks," he said. "Thanks for telling me the score. I'll get hold of Julio Cordovez. He can help if anyone can. But remember this: don't get yourself in a jam."

"I won't."

"That thirty-day law of theirs applies to you, too. But if you want to call the police and tell them you walked in and found him like this—" He hesitated as a new thought came. "Does anyone else know you had this date?"

"His secretary. I made it through her."

"Then it has to be that way," Jeff said. He released her hands and straightened up, some part of his conscience telling him that this was not the way but unable to find an alternative.

"I'll be on my way," he said. "You can telephone now if you like." He gave her a lopsided grin. "We seem to have an affinity for murder. Last night it was you and this time it's my turn."

"Wait!" The word came sharply as he turned away and now she came suddenly to her feet. "I just remembered," she breathed. "I came in a car and told the driver to wait. He's parked just outside. He'll be sure to see you."

"Oh, fine," Jeff said. "Well, it was a good idea while it lasted," he added resignedly, "and don't think I don't appreciate it."

If she paid any attention to this admission of failure she gave no visible sign. For a second her young face was grave with thought and then her eyes brightened and her lips parted.

"I know," she said. "You come with me and stay just inside the downstairs doorway. I'll tell the driver to go for a policeman and when he gets far enough away you can slip out. . . . Why not?" she demanded, obviously delighted with the suggestion, even if it was her own.

Jeff looked at her and sighed, marveling a little that anyone so lovely-looking could think so clearly under pressure. He understood also that the plan might work if his luck was in and a policeman didn't happen to be stationed too close to the door. And if his luck was out, what difference could it make?

"Sure," he said respectfully. "Let's give it a try," he said, and led the way through the office and down the darkened stairs.

11

KAREN HOLMES was a lot more worried than she cared to admit, even to herself, but she was excited too and confident that her plan would work. She felt Jeff's hand give her arm a final squeeze as he stood back in the doorway and then she was hurrying diagonally across the sidewalk to the taxi that had been parked with two wheels on the curb.

The driver sat up and touched his cap, smiling first and then blinking as she started to tell him what she wanted. Not until she saw his expression did she remember that he could not understand English.

"Oh, dear," she said to herself and then, putting down the quick surge of her consternation, she remembered a word, and then another.

"*Policía!*" she cried and pointed back to the doorway. "*Policía! . . . Pronto, pronto!*"

The words worked like magic and the expression on her face helped. The driver slid out of his seat and slammed the door. He glanced up and down the street and Karen said: "*Pronto!*" again as dramatically as she could, and then he wheeled and began to lope down the street.

People stopped to watch him and he called to them over his shoulder. While they watched him, she saw Jeff sidle out of the doorway and start in the opposite direction. Only then did she begin to breathe again and force herself to re-enter the half-light of the hall and start her climb.

She closed the office door behind her, telling herself she must not give in to the uncertainties that blotted out the excitement she had so recently felt. She had to think now, to prepare herself emotionally for what was to follow, to keep her poise as best she could. For she was certain that the story Jeff had told her must be true. She had seen enough of him on the plane coming to Miami to know the sort of person he was, and the things he had said last night in her room, even though he had the right to be bitter and angry with her, supported her original impression.

It helped now to realize that she was making up in part for the trick she had been forced to play on him at the Miami airport. But it was more than that and she knew it. She liked him. She liked him so much she wanted to help. The simple understanding of this made her feel good all over.

She went back to the doorway of the private office and glanced in, being careful to avoid Grayson but letting her eyes move slowly around the perimeter of the room. That was how she happened to notice the shiny object on the rug beneath the far corner of the desk. From where she stood she knew only that it was small and metallic-looking and then, moving closer and stooping to retrieve it, she saw that it had a yellow color that might have been gold. Shaped like a thimble, but having a polished rather than a dimpled surface, it resembled a tiny cup. Then, as she turned it over in her fingers, she heard the outer door open and close.

With no time to put the object in her bag, she thrust it into the front of her brassière and started for the doorway, expecting to find a policeman. Instead she saw a tanned, compactly built man in a cream-colored suit. His hair was a curly brown and close cut, his squarish face was hard muscled and thin at the mouth. He regarded her with narrowed unsmiling eyes as he advanced.

"*Buenas tardes,*" he said.

"Good afternoon," Karen said, knowing somehow that this must be Carl Webb, the man from Las Vegas.

"Oh? American?" His glance slid beyond her. "Is Grayson in?"

"In there," she said with a nod of her head. "He's dead."

She heard him say: "*He's what?*" as he stepped round her, and then she was following him into the office, watching him drop to one knee and make a quick inspection of the body. When he straightened he gave her a quick, hard stare and spoke one word that was profane and coldly cadenced.

His eyes busy now, he stepped to the desk and opened the attaché case. When he had pawed through the contents, he began to open and close the desk drawers, all of which were empty. By the time he had finished Karen heard the noise behind her. When she turned she saw the khaki-clad city policeman. He had one hand on the butt of his holstered gun. Behind him came the taxi driver.

Language difficulties reduced the next few minutes to a

lesson in pantomime. Already suspicious, the policeman drew his heavy revolver the moment he saw the body on the floor. He began to shout in Spanish until Webb cut him short.

"*¡No hable español!*" he shouted back.

The officer glared at them and was momentarily still as he considered his predicament. Then, gesturing with the gun, he made it clear he wanted them to move to the wall behind the desk. When they complied, he made a quick inspection of the body and then spoke rapidly to the open-mouthed taxi driver. The fellow got hold of himself and said: "*Si, si,*" and then he was dialing the telephone while the policeman shouted instructions and kept his eyes on his captives.

Quite oblivious of Karen, Carl Webb began to swear and the way he did it was not particularly offensive. The words were measured and distinct and spoken to himself. Not until he ran out of breath did he glance at her.

"I'm sorry," he said. "I had to get it out of my system." He pointed at her bag. "You wouldn't have it in there, would you?"

"Have what?"

"Cash. One hundred and twenty thousand bucks' worth."

Karen, certain now that her first guess had been right, said:

"You're Mr. Webb, aren't you?"

"How did you know?"

"Jeffrey Lane told me about you last night. . . . No, I don't have the cash; would you like to look?" She offered the white bag and watched Webb study it a moment, apparently estimating its size. Finally he shrugged and shook his head.

"How did the law get here?"

"I sent the taxi driver," Karen said and explained what

she had done. "I'm Karen Holmes," she said. "I was supposed to see Mr. Grayson at four o'clock and I came in and—"

"I heard about you," Webb said and for the first time gave her his attention. His glance moved openly from her legs to her face, which he inspected at some length. Apparently he liked what he saw. He gave her a small sardonic smile. "We both got gypped, hunh?" he said. "The only difference is—you've had it."

"Have I?"

"You came down to get some assignment," Webb said. "Did you get it?"

"No."

"And now you never will, right? I came for cash. I haven't got it but somebody has. I've still got a chance."

He stopped as two radio policemen hurried into the office. There was a lot of excited Spanish thrown around after that until, as had happened the night before, Ramon Zumeta arrived with another detective and the doctor. Presently the uniformed branch representing the city police left and Zumeta came over to Karen to find out what happened.

She gave a carefully worded account that she had rehearsed mentally. When she finished Webb added his own story. Zumeta nodded but asked no other questions.

"You can wait in the front room if you like," he said, and gestured to the detective, who accompanied them and then stood by while they sat down on the couch. Webb brought out a silver case, and Karen took the offered cigarette and a light. She placed her bag in her lap and leaned back, feeling now the pressure of the thimble between her breasts but not daring to squirm about and relieve that pressure.

When she saw the men come with the stretcher she closed her eyes. During the next few minutes she knew that

men were coming in and out of the office and once when
she put out her cigarette she saw that the stretcher-bearers
had gone with their burden. When Zumeta finally pulled
a chair in front of the couch she was ready for him.

"You came to see Mr. Grayson because you had made an
appointment with his secretary over the telephone," he
said. "What time was that, Miss Holmes?"

"The appointment? At four."

"But the call the police received did not come until four
thirty."

"Well—I may have been late getting here."

"The man who drove you here says no."

Oh—oh, she thought, and suddenly her apprehension
was mounting and she knew this was not going to be as
easy as she had imagined. Another look at Zumeta's steady
dark eyes told her he would be a difficult man to fool, and
now she knew she had to think—and think fast.

"Oh," she said. "I see what you mean."

She gave him a smile that she hoped seemed confident.
She asked, and answered, a lot of silent questions in an
effort to bolster her courage and her wits.

She was the one who had wanted to be the private detective, wasn't she? She had bullied her father for his per-
mission, hadn't she? She had griped about the routine
dullness of her assignments? Yes, yes, yes!

Well, then, Karen my girl, act the part!

This is what she told herself, and suddenly she was talking, hoping her father might be proud of what she was doing even if she had broken the law and was now offering
a series of lies she hoped would substantiate her original
premise.

"I didn't know he was in there," she said. "I didn't think
anyone was here."

"But you waited."

"Naturally." She fluttered one hand. "I had this appoint-

ment and I thought Mr. Grayson must have stepped out
because the door was unlocked. I sat right here." She
patted the cushion at her side. "I waited—until I began to
wonder how long it would be— I suppose I got restless,"
she said.

"That is understandable."

"So I looked around." She pointed at the carton near the
desk with its load of discarded papers. "I could tell someone was moving out and—well—I took a peek in that next
office." She tried another little smile, making sure Zumeta
saw it. She put a note of shy confession in her voice. "I
suppose I just got curious," she said. "I went on to the last
office and—there he was.

"I don't know what I did then," she said, making her
tone hushed, "or how long I was there. At first I didn't
know what the matter was. I couldn't make myself touch
him and then I knew I had to do something. I tried to
shake him and finally I knew I should run and get help."
She folded her hands and dropped her glance. "That's
what I did," she said, pleased with the story that she had
brought out of nowhere and silently defying him to refute
it.

Zumeta did not try. He cleared his throat and turned to
Webb, asking first for his tourist card.

She watched him unfold the paper and give it a quick
glance.

"Carl Webb," he said. "A tourist. From Las Vegas,
Nevada." Zumeta returned the paper and asked if Webb
had heard about Harry Baker. When Webb nodded,
Zumeta said: "Baker went to Barbados. He sent some
cables to Las Vegas. We have those cables."

"I have some, too," Webb said and produced four sheets.

Zumeta read them. When he looked up his dark gaze was
thoughtful and intent. "You came to collect this money
from Baker?"

"That's right," Webb said. "I might have made it if the goddamned plane hadn't been late."

"And you came here this afternoon. Why?"

"I had a date."

"You have seen Mr. Grayson previous to this?"

"Just before noon."

"You threatened him?"

"I didn't have to. He knew the score. He said he'd have the cash for me this afternoon."

"Ah-h," said Zumeta. "But you did not get it." He glanced at Karen. "You did not find it here?"

"No."

"So." Zumeta's big shoulders moved in a faint shrug. "That is too bad for you, Mr. Webb."

"What?"

"It occurs to me that with Mr. Grayson dead the money is no longer his to give but the property of the widow. When it is located it will be hers."

"Yeah?" Webb's mouth compressed and his bright gaze was challenging. "Not if I find it first."

There was something in the flat, even tone that told Karen Webb meant just what he said, and when she glanced at Zumeta she saw his eyes open and close while things happened behind them. His mouth twisted at one corner as he pushed his chair back and stood up.

"In that case," he said, "I can only caution you to be most careful, Mr. Webb. We have a model prison here at San Juan de los Morros but it is still a prison. . . . We will go now to my office," he said. "I will send for Mrs. Grayson. Perhaps she can help us."

12

THE CITY'S newest hotel, the Tamanaco, stood perched on a hillside some distance from the center of town. It had a sloping modern look, not in the boxlike tradition of some Jeff had seen, but with a style of its own that might have been influenced by ancient Indian architecture. From a distance it had reminded him of things that had been done by the Incas, but seen close-up the resemblance disappeared and it became a plush, expensive-looking hostelry with all the latest in décor and conveniences.

The public rooms were spacious and airy and spread over two floors, the lower of which gave on a wide expanse of lawn, cabanas, the usual umbrella-shaded tables, and an impressive, oddly shaped pool complete with diving tower. Jeff walked through the lobby to the veranda overlooking the terrace. When he caught a waiter's eye he asked for a gin and tonic and took a chair near the railing. Not until then did he realize how weary he was; not until then did he feel that, temporarily at least, he was safe.

It had bothered him greatly as he hurried from Grayson's office. Clad as he was in gabardine slacks and a cord coat, he was acutely conscious of the fact that he looked not only like a tourist but like an American tourist. He did not know how long it would be before someone would connect him with the murder; and—once the word was out that he was wanted for questioning—he would be noticed by every plainclothes detective he passed.

He could not go back to the Tucan, nor did he dare wait

for Julio Cordovez in any downtown bar lest he seem conspicuous. He thought once of the American Club, but this also seemed too obvious, so when he telephoned the little detective's office he left word for Cordovez to look for him here. What he needed was protective coloring, and since most of the Tamanaco guests were from the States, he could move freely here without attracting attention.

He was still working on his drink when a chair moved beside him and Cordovez slid into it, not looking at him at first but giving his attention to the still-colorful spectacle at the poolside.

"Beer?" Jeff said.

"*Gracias.*"

Jeff signaled the waiter, ordering the beer and a refill for himself. "I'm in a jam," he said. "*¿Entiende?*"

"*Sí.*"

"My stepbrother got himself killed this afternoon."

Cordovez was still watching the acrobats in the water but he sucked in his breath with a small whistling sound.

"Is bad," he said. "How does this happen?"

Jeff waited until the waiter had been taken care of and then he told what he knew and what he had done. Still impassive but nodding from time to time, Cordovez sipped his beer and made no comment until the story had been told. What he said first surprised Jeff even though he agreed with the comment.

"This girl you speak of has much spirit," he said approvingly."But for her you would now be at *Segurnal.*"

"I might be invited to stay, too."

"This is true. The fight you had, the marks on your hand, the bloodstain I noticed—all this would be difficult to explain." He put his beer glass aside and stood up. "If you will excuse me, I will make a telephone call."

Jeff frowned as he watched the little man go and then the frown went away and he took a breath. The thought of this phone call worried him as he considered it, but not for long. He had already committed himself. Either Cordovez was on his side and would remain so, or he was taking the first step at resigning his job. He lit a cigarette and waited. Presently Cordovez returned and picked up his glass. As though there had been no interruption he said:

"You have no idea who has taken the money?"

"None."

"But you think Señor Baker was murdered because of it?"

"I don't know what else to think."

"But if the man from Nevada—"

"Webb."

"If he tells the truth it would seem that Grayson thought to have this money for him last night. By then the money is gone but perhaps Grayson has an idea who took it."

He paused and sipped more beer. He wiped his mouth. "Today he demands its return and the thief will not give it up. To make sure Grayson can never tell on him, he makes this attack."

Jeff did not argue the premise. He was thinking ahead, knowing there were at least two people he had to talk to but worrying now about where he could stay until he had a chance to make his inquiries. Not until then did he face up to the unpleasant knowledge that he not only was on the run, but he also had to hide. He said as much to Cordovez and the detective nodded.

"That is true and it will not be easy. *Segurnal* is everywhere. Me, I can often tell those men even when I do not know them, but for you it is more difficult. You can never know which man works for Pedro Vidal. They work when necessary as waiters, as taxi drivers, doormen, behind counters at bars. *Segurnal* has many ears and long arms."

"If I could get a room in some small hotel—"

"A hotel is no good," Cordovez said emphatically.

"Why not?"

"The good ones require your tourist card and you must fill out papers. The others"—he shrugged—"are already under observation. This you must believe."

"Great," Jeff said. He drained his glass and put it aside with a nervous gesture. "What do I do, sleep in the park or hide in the hills?"

Cordovez chuckled and showed his teeth. "It is all arranged. You will stay at my place."

Jeff looked at him and the sudden glow he felt inside him came not from alcohol but from gratitude. He looked down at his drink, his lean face relaxing. He considered again the simple statement and when he glanced up his gaze was warm and friendly.

"Thanks, Julio," he said and shook his head. "But it's no good."

"But of course. That was why I made the telephone call. My wife has a sister on the other side of the city. This sister has a husband more prosperous than Julio Cordovez and the house is large." He glanced at his strapwatch. "Already my wife will have the two children dressed and ready for the trip."

Jeff regarded him with growing wonderment and respect, knowing what he said must be true. Such openhanded hospitality made him more deeply appreciative, but in his own mind this was an imposition he could not take lightly and he felt compelled to voice his objection.

"It's very kind of you, Julio," he said, "but I don't think you should risk it. If *Segurnal* is as good as you say, it's just a question of time before they nail me. When they do you'll be in a jam."

"I am already in this jam you speak of for not informing on you now. . . . No," Cordovez said flatly, "it is better that you do as Julio says. And who knows, we may have our solution before *Segurnal* can pick you up. It is the only way. You have an idea perhaps?" he asked hopefully.

"A couple," Jeff said. "I think Dan Spencer was blackmailing my stepbrother. From what I saw in Arnold's checkbook, he'd been paying Spencer three hundred bolivars a week for quite a while."

"Ah," said Cordovez softly. "You think Spencer knew of your stepbrother's secret debt in the state of Nevada?"

"Baker was a cop in Las Vegas," Jeff said. "He worked for the same hotel as my stepbrother. He must have known all about Arnold and when he located him here he knew why Arnold was hiding. Furthermore, Arnold trusted him enough to hire him to send those cables from Barbados. Apparently he was supposed to make the payment to Webb."

"That I understand."

"But Spencer once worked for a newspaper in Las Vegas. He knew Baker; he also knew my stepbrother. Some time ago he must have run into him here and Arnold must have decided to put him on the payroll to make sure Spencer didn't write the Las Vegas crowd what he knew."

"Yes," Cordovez said. "And you will wish to verify this with Spencer?"

"Right," Jeff said. "But first I'd like to have a talk with Luis Miranda."

"Miranda?" Cordovez's brows climbed as his eyes opened. "Miranda?" he said again in the first display of surprise Jeff had ever witnessed. "But if you think Señor Baker was killed for money—and Grayson too—then Luis Miranda would not do this. He would not need the money, even in that amount."

"Do you know his wife's name?"

Cordovez blinked at the digression. "His wife?" He frowned. "No, I do not."

Jeff took the two airplane tickets from his pocket and

passed them over. He waited while the detective studied them carefully and when Cordovez returned them his face held a strange expression.

"I had heard it said that your stepbrother and this woman were friendly," he said finally. "I have heard that Luis Miranda is a jealous man. Still—"

He let the sentence dangle, sighed, and pushed back his chair. "Very well," he said. "We will go. At this hour he may still be at his office. My car is outside."

Julio Cordovez found a parking place across the street from the entrance of this towering office building that, had its walls sloped slightly, would have resembled a multi-windowed obelisk. His smooth face held a worried look as he turned off the motor, and before Jeff could get out he offered a word of caution and a suggestion.

"Luis Miranda is a proud man," he said. "A dangerous man to insult, with a temper that is quick. I do not know what will happen when you speak of his wife—if that is your intention—but I do not think it wise for you to go to his office."

"Why?"

"To explain your position or to ask for any assistance you will first have to speak of this new murder. Who can say how he will react?"

"I don't know," Jeff said, "but if I don't go, how do I get to talk to him? It's a chance I have to take."

"But if there is a better way?"

"Is there?"

"His office is on what floor?"

"Fourteen."

"And when you have finished your talk, what is to prevent him from picking up the telephone to report your presence to the police? The radio cars come quick these days. If there should be any delay in waiting for an elevator you could be picked up at the entrance before you could reach my car. If you do not mind a suggestion I think it best to try another way."

Jeff had been paying attention and what Cordovez said made sense.

"I'm listening," he said.

"First I will see if he is in his office. If so I will wait downstairs until he comes out. I will then say you wish to see him and if he agrees I will bring him here and you can talk. If I have any doubts we will have to think of something else but no harm will be done for the moment."

He smiled again as Jeff hesitated, then opened the car door. From the top of the sun visor he removed a newspaper printed in Spanish. "If you pretend to read this," he said, "your face will be well hidden."

It was exactly eighteen minutes later when Jeff saw them start across the street, Miranda immaculately erect in his dark suit and Panama hat, Cordovez bareheaded, his bald spot glistening in the fading sunlight, trotting a little to keep pace. As they neared the car Jeff replaced the newspaper and gave the detective proper credit for a smart idea, well executed; then he stepped out on the sidewalk and waited.

Miranda nodded coldly, his black eyes speculating. "I do not understand why you did not come to my office," he said. "But if you wish to talk here I can spare you five minutes."

"You will be more comfortable in back," Cordovez said, and opened the rear door. "I will wait near by."

Miranda slid over on the seat and Jeff followed him; the confidence he had felt earlier was dissipating rapidly, but he was determined to find out what he could while he could. He asked first if Miranda knew about Arnold Grayson.

"I was informed by the police fifteen minutes ago," Miranda said. "You wish to talk to me because you feel the need of legal counsel?"

"Not exactly," Jeff said. "But it's something I may need a lot of before too long and I might as well tell you what I know."

There was no interruption as he related the facts as he knew them. He pointed out his own position as a suspect but made no mention of Karen Holmes's part in making his present freedom possible.

"Because you had this fight with Grayson, and because Spencer may have seen you come from the building, you decided to run," Miranda said. "You are afraid the police are now looking for you. And what do you expect to gain by this?"

"Time," Jeff said, "and maybe some information." Then, because he knew of no other way, he plunged ahead, his body poised should he need to move quickly. "Because the way I see it you have a pretty fair motive for murder yourself, Mr. Miranda."

He could feel the other stiffen beside him but when there was no immediate reply, he said: "What is your wife's first name?"

"Muriel."

"And what would you say if I told you she was planning to run away with Grayson tomorrow night?"

The brown, aristocratic face grew pale at the cheekbones and the answer came quickly, the words clipped and forceful.

"I would demand that you prove your accusation or apologize instantly."

Jeff already had the two airline tickets in his hand and he passed them quickly to Miranda without comment. He watched the man's dark gaze narrow as he examined the covers of the two tickets. He sat that way for several seconds, as though reluctant to open them and see what lay inside. Finally he bent one cover back, glanced at the ticket; he examined the other. He looked at Jeff.

"Where did you get them?"

Jeff told him. "If there's any doubt in your mind," he said, "you could check with the airline office. The only point that concerns me is—did you know about this or didn't you?"

The outburst Jeff had expected never came. There was no denial, no outward sign that Miranda had heard what was said. He settled back against the cushions, no longer looking at Jeff or the tickets. His gaze was fixed at some point beyond the windshield, but the things he saw were in his mind. When he spoke, his voice had a remote quality and the thoughts he expressed came from the past.

"It has never been easy," he said.

Jeff hesitated, and then checked the question that came to mind, as some instinctive knowledge warned him not to break the spell Miranda had cast about himself.

"She could not get used to the customs of this country," he added finally. "She had always had much freedom and she could not understand that here a wife does not go out in the evening without her husband. In the afternoon, perhaps with other women to tea, yes; not otherwise.

"She worked at the Tamanaco," he said. "She was brought here because she was experienced in hotel work —as a secretary and a hostess. There are many cocktail parties given there for business reasons. She would arrange the details. That is how I met her. After that I saw her as often as I could because I knew then I wanted her for my wife. There was much I could give her. I think she knew this just as she knew that I loved her very much even though I was twenty years older.

"But as Mrs. Luis Miranda she had certain duties and obligations. I tried to explain these, to tell her that a woman was judged by standards different from those in the States. When I insisted, she accused me of being jealous—which I must admit I was—and of being too strict. She complained that she had no fun. She threatened to leave me, but without money I knew she would not do this since this also was important to her."

He fell silent, his gaze still remote and his dark face impassive. When the silence began to build, Jeff risked a question.

"You knew about Grayson?"

"Yes, I knew. He was a client. There were parties we both attended. But I did not know how friendly they had become." He paused again, and when he continued, the absent quality was missing from his voice and the accent was grim. "I have a beach cottage at Macuto, which is near the sea beyond La Guaira. I learned that there were afternoons when she had gone there with Grayson."

"You told her what you knew?"

"Naturally."

"You fought about it."

"There was no fight."

"But you were jealous," Jeff pressed, certain now that there would be no more reminiscing.

"I have admitted this."

"Grayson was beaten pretty savagely. It was the sort of attack a jealous husband would make. As a motive for murder you've got one of the best."

Miranda eyed him narrowly, watching intently, waiting.

"You thought you were going to lose your wife," Jeff said, "and that was something you were too proud to take. You made up your mind to handle Grayson in your own way. You went up to his office this afternoon and did just that."

"I agree that to have done so would have given me much pleasure," Miranda said frankly. "But did I also go to the room of Harry Baker and kill him too?" he asked with heavy irony.

"You were there."

"Where?"

"At the hotel. You were there at that party and it would have been a cinch to duck out long enough to go upstairs. You knew Grayson had raised the cash. You knew why."

Miranda laughed abruptly and sat up, his smile thin and mirthless, his tone deprecating.

"If you had the time I would give you a letter to my bankers, Mr. Lane," he said. "I believe they could assure you that this money you speak of would hardly tempt me."

The comment stopped Jeff momentarily and the argument he offered sounded inadequate, even to him.

"Even the rich get hard up for cash sometimes."

"Possibly," Miranda said, "but it occurs to me that you also have an excellent motive for murder. You were worried about losing control of your company, is this not so? You were afraid that your stepbrother would vote his stock with the opposition. Now you have no worries. You and your sister will have this stock for yourselves because your stepbrother is dead.

"It can be proved that you hated him, I think. You went to his office to threaten him and there was violence between you." His smile was fixed as he reached for the door handle. "But this I will do for you, Mr. Lane. I disliked your stepbrother intensely even though I handled some of his affairs. What has happened this afternoon has removed a serious problem for me. So I will do this: when you are arrested, and I do not think it will be too long now, I will be happy to defend you for nothing."

He opened the door, pulled himself erect, and bowed stiffly. As he started to turn away, Jeff thought of one more question.

"Did my stepbrother leave a will?"

"Not that I know of."

"Then his wife will inherit."

"It would seem so."

He bowed again and this time he wheeled and continued up the street, his shoulders back, his Panama centered on his well-shaped head.

13

JULIO CORDOVEZ made no comment as he started the car and pulled out into the traffic stream. Dusk had begun to finger the sidewalks now and here and there a light winked on in some store window. When they came to a traffic circle that was temporarily jammed, Julio shifted into neutral and said:

"Luis Miranda was helpful?"

"Not very," Jeff said unhappily.

"You think he knew of the tickets to New York?"

Jeff roused himself sufficiently to consider the question. In his own mind the interview with Miranda had been singularly discouraging. He had not known exactly what he had expected to prove by it, but it had seemed like a good idea at the time. Now, ticking off the results, and omitting speculation, he saw that all he had actually learned was a little something about the background of Miranda's marriage, his feeling for his wife, and his—Miranda's—knowledge of her association with Grayson, all of which he had suspected. The only fact to come out of the discussion was the announcement that Grayson's wife would probably inherit his estate.

"I don't know if he actually knew," he said, "but he must have suspected something like that *might* happen. What I'd like to find out is whether Diana Grayson suspected the same thing."

"Luis Miranda would not steal the money," Cordovez said.

"You said that before," Jeff said, an unwanted edge in his voice.

"I'm sorry," Cordovez said. "I did not mean—"

"No, I'm sorry," Jeff said, a little ashamed because he had snapped at his friend. "Don't pay any attention to me," he said. "I'm in a lousy mood."

"A drink will help," Cordovez said cheerfully, "and some food. But first we will go to my place."

Jeff slumped back in the seat, observing the passing scene, but no longer having any idea where he was, until Cordovez pulled the car to the curb in front of an apartment house on the steep slope of a side street.

"Is this it?" he asked.

"No," Cordovez replied. "A friend. If you will wait I will not be long."

Jeff twisted his body far enough to get a cigarette out and when he had a light he stayed slumped, his eyes brooding and his mouth slack as the black mood of his depression settled more heavily about him. He did not stir when Cordovez opened the door. Not until he realized that the detective had brought something with him did he glance round to find Cordovez putting a suit on its hanger on the back seat and then placing a neatly folded white shirt on top of it.

"It should fit," Cordovez said as he slid behind the wheel.

"What?"

"The suit. It is for you."

"Me? But what—"

"I will explain," Cordovez said and chuckled at Jeff's

reaction. "I do not mean to criticize," he added. "The clothes you now wear are very fine, but too—shall we say —American. In the daytime it is less important, but after dark the successful Venezuelan wears a suit here in Caracas."

"Oh," Jeff said, impressed by the little detective's thoughtfulness and sagacity.

"Yes. With your dark hair and eyes you will pass for a citizen. With the proper suit it will be more difficult for the ears and arms of Pedro Vidal to penetrate this disguise. Also, you yourself will feel more secure and that, too, is important."

"Amen," said Jeff.

"Pardon?"

"What I meant was, I'm very glad I hired you."

"Me, too," said Cordovez and settled back to concentrate on his driving. . . .

The apartment house they came to presently was new-looking and three stories high. It contained six flats and Cordovez occupied the middle floor on the right side. Verandas had been recessed into the sides of the building instead of at the front, and inside the layout proved to be the railroad type—living-room, kitchen, and dinette, a hall from which opened a bedroom, bath, and bedroom.

The living-room was rather sparsely furnished but spotless, the curtains clean, the children's toys neatly piled in one corner. A small bed and a crib, visible from the doorway of the first bedroom, testified to its use. Cordovez was snapping on the light in the rear room.

"You will sleep here tonight," he said, indicating the double bed.

"And where will you sleep?"

"In the front room."

"Oh, no."

"But yes," Cordovez said firmly. "I will explain why. For one your size, the sofa will be uncomfortable. For me it serves very well. Believe me, I have tried it often. Come," he said, as though the matter was decided. "Try on the suit. Let us see if it will become you."

He slipped the coat and trousers from the hanger and unbuttoned the clean shirt while Jeff undressed. "My friend is about your size," he said. "You will find the coat somewhat different in cut to your own, but that is good. One noticing it will be assured it was manufactured in Caracas."

The shirt proved to be adequate, the sleeves a little short but the collar fitting perfectly. Jeff needed his belt to secure the waistband of the trousers, but the coat hung well and the shade of blue was inconspicuous.

"You see," Cordovez said happily.

He stood back. He spread his hands, and the expression on his face could have been no more pleased had he designed the suit himself.

"Dressed that way you look better. How does it feel?"

"Feels O. K.," Jeff said and began to transfer his things from his slacks and jacket to the new suit.

"Since I will do the talking," Cordovez said, "no one will suspect you are not a countryman of mine. Now, if you are ready," he said, "we will eat."

Once in the car, Cordovez went round the block and turned downhill. Still without knowing where he was, Jeff was again reminded of Southern California when the valley opened up and he saw the patternless brilliance of the lights and neon signs. He had the feeling that he had seen this part of the city in daylight but he did not recognize the triangular plaza where Cordovez parked the car.

"I hope you will like this," he said as he locked the doors. "There are three choices: Grilled meat, of many kinds and in small pieces; steak, which is usually good; and chicken, which is always dependable."

"How's the chicken fixed?"

"Grilled, like the others. You will see for yourself."

He led the way into a low-ceilinged room that was crowded, smoke-filled, and noisy. A trio consisting of accordion, violin, and bass played loudly and with gusto, and at first glance every table seemed taken. Then, at the steps which led to the adjacent room, Cordovez exchanged *Holas* with one of the proprietors. Words were spoken and a waiter dispatched to clean up a recently vacated place along the wall.

"Now," said Cordovez, settling himself, "you would like the chicken? And a salad?"

"And a drink."

"Yes."

"Whisky," Jeff said. "With a little soda. Tell the man a double whisky."

Cordovez conferred with the waiter, who was putting out knives, forks, and spoons of the kitchen variety. By the time Jeff had his cigarette going the whisky came and so did a beer for the detective.

"*Salud,*" he said, and raised his glass. He drank thirstily and wiped his mouth. He took out his notebook and ripped out a clean sheet, wrote down an address with his mechanical pencil, and passed the slip to Jeff.

"This is the address where I live," he said, "in case you need it to show to some taxi driver. Also"—he took a key from his pocket—"this is an extra key. My house is yours and you can come and go as you like."

"Until Pedro Vidal's boys pick me up," Jeff said dryly.

"Let us hope this does not happen— Ah-h." The dark eyes opened and the white teeth flashed in a smile of anticipation as he unfolded his paper napkin and eyed the food.

Jeff smiled in eager anticipation, too, not so much because he was hungry but because he had never seen anything quite like this. For when Cordovez said the food was grilled he meant just that, and on an individual basis. Each table had its own small grill and the charcoal was still smoldering when the waiter whisked it in front of them. On top of the grill a chicken had been split and rested with the skin up, a golden brown now and glistening with some clear sauce faintly flavored with onion.

To complete the presentation, individual cutting-boards were placed in front of them, instead of plates, to make the dismantling of the chicken easier. After that came the French fried potatoes in a basket, the hot bread, and a salad that was aromatic and crisply cool.

"You like this place?" Cordovez asked when he had licked his fingers and dried them on the napkin.

"Very much," Jeff said. "The food was delicious."

Cordovez accepted a cigarette and gave forth with a contented sigh. He glanced about the room and then, as though once more conscious of the problem which still had to be faced, his expression grew serious.

"What would you like to do now?"

Reluctantly Jeff brought his thoughts into focus. He wanted most to have a talk with Dan Spencer, but he was afraid to go to the newspaper office, and he knew that since the *Bulletin* was a morning paper, it would be some time before Spencer was off duty. Meanwhile—

"I'd like to talk to Mrs. Grayson again if you think we can manage it."

"We can try. The house is not far from here," Cordovez said, but later, as the car rolled slowly up the winding street in second gear, he offered some words of caution.

"I will not stop now," he said as they approached the low and rambling house and saw the light in the windows. "I wish to make sure no one is watching."

He pressed the clutch pedal and their momentum carried them past the driveway and now Cordovez had his head out the window and his nose in the air, as though he was trying to find some scent of danger. He drove on another block and turned round. He passed the house again with his lights out and pulled a hundred feet beyond the crest of the hill.

"You will not need me inside?"

"No."

"I think it is safe, but it is also better that I wait here. If you hear the horn three times you will know there is some difficulty. In that event it might be best for you to leave by the back entrance—if you can."

Jeff got out and closed the door quietly. He said there wasn't going to be any trouble and that all Julio had to do was sit and take a little snooze.

14

DUDLEY FISKE opened the door in response to Jeff's ring. When he recognized his caller his eyes blinked uncertainly behind the glasses and he stood in the opening, one hand still on the knob.

"Oh, hello, Lane," he said without enthusiasm. "Aren't you taking a bit of a chance coming here?"

"Why?" Jeff said. "Are you thinking of turning me in?"

"It's not that. It's just that I understood the police were looking for you. They've been here before and I wouldn't be surprised if they came back."

"I'd like to talk to Mrs. Grayson," Jeff said. "It shouldn't take too long."

Again Fiske seemed undecided, but now a woman's voice called to him from some inner room and this apparently decided him. He moved aside. Jeff waited until he had closed the door and then waited for Fiske to lead the way.

"After you," he said, "if you don't mind."

If Diana Grayson was suffering emotionally over the loss of her husband, she gave no outward sign of the tragedy. Her gray hair shone softly in the lamplight and her blue dress with its tight bodice and flaring skirt seemed more suitable for an afternoon party at the Tamanaco. She had a cigarette in one hand, a brandy snifter in the other, and when she saw Jeff she waved at the tray on the coffee table with its bottle and glasses. A similar glass, still partly full, stood to one side.

"Come in, Mr. Lane," she said. "Will you have a brandy?"

"Thanks, no," Jeff said, uncertain now just how to proceed and finally settling for the conventional way. He started to say he was sorry to break in like this at such a time, but she cut him off before he could finish.

"It's quite all right," she said. "I stopped being hypocritical about most things some time ago. You must know from what was said this morning how I felt about your stepbrother. What happened this afternoon shocked me. I'm sure it would shock anyone. No one wanted to live more than Arnold, and I do feel sorry for him, but I can't pretend that I feel something that he killed a long time ago. I simply no longer have that capacity. There was something about him that was evil and in the end it destroyed him."

Remembering Luis Miranda's phrase about the evil man,

Jeff glanced at Dudley Fiske, who had been standing to one side and now shifted his weight.

"I think he wants to talk to you, Di," he said and reached down to pick up his glass. "I'll run along to my rooms until you've finished."

"I'd rather you stayed," Jeff said, moving slightly to block the man's progress.

Fiske stopped and it occurred to Jeff that this was not the same man he had seen that morning. This man had no easy smile, his gaze was steady and unfriendly as it measured Jeff. His voice was challenging rather than apologetic.

"Why?" he demanded.

"Because I wouldn't want you to duck out and call the police."

Fiske put his glass down and squared his shoulders. For a second or two they stood that way, glances locked, Jeff the taller and more vital-looking of the two, Fiske the heavier but more poorly conditioned. Then, as though to prove that the change Jeff had noticed was to be a permanent thing, he said, his voice quietly ominous:

"Do you think you can stop me?"

"I can try."

"Without a club?"

"Club?" Jeff peered at him.

"That's what was used on Arnold, so the police say. A club or a cane."

"Oh, stop it!"

Diana Grayson put her glass down with a bang and her voice was clipped and impatient.

"Sit down, Dudley," she said. "Please." She waited until Fiske obeyed her and then she looked at Jeff, one dark brow arched. "I don't blame you for being concerned," she said, "but I think you misjudge Dudley. He's not after vengeance, you know, and neither am I. What happened, happened. It's over and done with and so far as I am con-

cerned the only genuine feeling I have at the moment is
one of relief."

Jeff believed her. The odds had finally caught up with
Arnold Grayson and there was no one to mourn his passing; it was as simple as that. What this woman had said
did not shock him because he knew his stepbrother too
well. But her frankness, though not entirely unexpected,
made him reconsider his tactics, and when his glance again
touched the brandy bottle, he changed his mind about the
drink. He poured an ounce or so into the glass, swished it
around as he took a chair near the end of the divan. He
did not give it the connoisseur's routine but finished it in
two small swallows.

"Miranda had a different way of putting it," he said.

"Miranda?" Both brows arched this time and her surprise seemed genuine. "Luis? You have seen him?"

"Late this afternoon," Jeff said. "I can't remember his
exact words, but what he meant was that things were a
lot simpler for him with Arnold out of the way. Tell me,"
he said, "did you know he planned to fly to New York
tomorrow night and take Muriel Miranda with him?"

"Who planned?"

"Your husband."

For a long moment then she sat immobile, her face still.
She was sitting with her knees crossed and arms folded
lightly across her bosom and while Jeff waited she let her
hands come down. Her head turned slightly so she could
see Fiske. What happened to her eyes in that instant Jeff
could not guess but when she again gave him her attention
her voice was composed.

"I don't believe it."

Jeff produced the tickets and tossed them on the divan.
He watched her inspect first one and then the other before
she pushed them away from her.

"You didn't know about this?" he persisted.

"Naturally not."

"And if you had?"

"I'm sure I don't know," she said sullenly. "I could hardly hold him here bodily."

Fiske stirred in his chair. "What difference does it make, Lane?" he said with some belligerence. "You heard her say she didn't know. Isn't that good enough?"

Jeff ignored him, and continued to the woman: "Miranda says there was no will. He says you will inherit whatever Arnold had. Do you know how much that will be?"

"For one thing, this house," she said. "It's the only thing left in both our names." She paused, head tipping slightly as she considered her answer. I suppose there's some money in his bank account. Two cars, the furniture. I don't know anything about his business affairs."

"Fiske does," Jeff said. "He was the assistant." He regarded the man a silent moment. "When were you in the office last?"

"This morning, not that it's any of your business."

"Then you knew he was cleaning out the place."

"How do you know?" Fiske asked suspiciously. "Where did you get those tickets?"

Touché, Jeff thought, and reminded himself to be more careful with his questions.

He was not ready to admit he had seen Grayson that afternoon, but the fact remained that the office had been cleaned out and Fiske could not help knowing it. He might even have known about the two airplane tickets. That someone was lying seemed obvious, but because it also seemed pointless to pursue that line of reasoning, he ignored the question and said:

"That hundred and twenty thousand in cash would be part of the estate, wouldn't it? Assuming that it is recovered? I mean, there's no reason now why you'd have to turn it over to Carl Webb."

Diana made an impatient throaty sound. "I should say not," she said. "That was Arnold's little project, not mine."

"You knew he had raised this cash. You knew he intended to pay off so he could go back to the States."

"Well, yes," she admitted, grudgingly, it seemed.

"But *you* had made no plans for returning."

"I'm making plans now," she said, not bothering to deny the statement. "I'm going to put this house on the market. I'll sell the cars and the furniture. I'm going back just as soon as I can and Dudley"—she glanced at Fiske and a suggestion of a smile softened the lines of her mouth—"is going with me."

The same idea had already occurred to Jeff, and having seen these two together before, he could accept the announcement. Twice Diana Grayson had been married and both times happiness had escaped her. Through Grayson's neglect and indifference she had come to know Fiske and to find in him a certain loyalty and devotion she had never experienced before.

There was no way of telling how long this relationship had existed, but the understanding was there, and the change that had come over Fiske, now that this understanding was out in the open, seemed not only obvious but beneficial. With the way cleared for him he had miraculously acquired a confidence and purpose entirely lacking in his performance earlier that afternoon when Arnold Grayson was still alive. Through this woman's acceptance of him he had attained his majority as a man. Now he was ready to do what he had to do to protect his newfound gains.

How long Fiske's desire had lain dormant Jeff did not bother to guess, but he understood now that here was a motive for murder quite beside the hundred and twenty thousand in cash. The money could have been the factor that triggered their actions and brought them both to the

Hotel Tucan the night before. It was an amount which represented more than half of Grayson's estate and it occurred to Jeff that Diana seemed oddly complacent about its loss—if indeed there had been a loss.

He could not see how she could have killed either Baker or her husband, but she could have been involved as the instigator. She had stayed in the car, according to Cordovez, while Fiske prowled about the hotel. Both knew that he, Jeff, had left here this afternoon to see Grayson at his office. But remembering the blue tinge on that face and the welts that marked it, he could not believe she could have made them, not unless she had been able to knock him unconscious with the first blow. What had been done to Grayson had been done by a man.

Why not Fiske? He had the motive, he could have made the opportunity. If he needed an alibi, the woman could supply it.

Yet even as these thoughts came to Jeff he knew it would do no good to voice them. He could accuse and they could deny. He had no proof and could think of no way of getting any. His own accomplishment was the understanding of the relationship of these two which made possible a motive for murder he had not considered before. But he was through for the moment and he knew it.

He stood up and Fiske rose with him, his round face relieved but his bespectacled gaze revealing no uncertainty. He nodded to the woman and thanked her for the brandy. To Fiske he said:

"If you want to call the police when I leave it's O. K. with me."

"I don't think we will," Diana said. "They'll only come and clutter up the place, and as I said before I don't think either of us is in a vengeful mood. Good night, Mr. Lane."

Julio Cordovez stepped on the starter when Jeff opened

the car door and this time, as they started to roll downhill, Jeff spoke of the things that had been said, his voice a monotone of dejection.

"Yes," Cordovez said when the information had been given. "It is discouraging, but it is good that you came. If you had not done so you would not understand this man and this woman. As you say, you have no proof, but you now have a motive that did not exist for you before. . . . You wish to see Dan Spencer?"

"Yeah," Jeff said. "If you can find a telephone maybe you can get an idea when he should be through."

They were in the valley now and presently Cordovez pulled into a gas station. When he had given his order to the attendant he disappeared inside.

"Spencer will be finished by midnight and perhaps before," he announced when he came back. "It is now ten minutes after eleven."

"Let's go," Jeff said. And later, as they approached the downtown section, he roused himself and said: "I think I'll handle this one alone."

"As you wish."

"You go down to *Segurnal* and see what happened there this afternoon. See if you can find out how they're figuring this one. Also—"

"Yes?" Cordovez said when Jeff hesitated.

"I'd like you to see Miss Holmes and tell her I'll be at your place in case she wants to get in touch with me."

"You think this is wise?"

"If you mean can I trust her—yes. I wouldn't be here now if it wasn't for her."

"That is true."

"She knows I didn't kill Grayson and I think she'd like to help if she can. She might know something we don't. You can explain it. What I mean is"—Jeff paused because he was not exactly sure just what he meant and could find

no good reason for his concern—"if she doesn't know anything, tell her to keep away from me. I don't want her to
get in any trouble on my account. But if she should know
something—"

"I understand."

Cordovez made a turn into a narrow hillside street.

"I will let you out at the corner," he said, "and point
out the proper building. You will want to wait near by,
but I would not stand in one place too long."

"Oh?"

"The city police are not as smart as the *oficiales* of
Segurnal but one could become curious."

"I'll watch it," Jeff said as the car stopped at the intersection. He followed Cordovez's pointing finger and located the doorway to the *Bulletin* halfway down the block.
"See you back at your place," he said, and then moved
into the shadows, walking downhill and keeping to the
curb.

It was quieter now. Cars were still parked on one side,
but the few pedestrians were faceless individuals in the
darkness and the doorways he passed were obscure. Opposite the newspaper he stopped to let his eyes become
accustomed to the darkness. He could see a front office
through the barred and open windows on the street floor.
Light glowed more brightly from some room beyond, and
far back in the adjacent hall he could make out the rolls
of newsprint.

He found a cigarette and lit it, standing now so that he
faced the street. Footsteps coming downhill made him turn
his head. A man and woman, walking close together and
speaking softly, passed behind him and presently the silence came again. It had a strange, narcotic effect on his
senses so that he was not aware of any sound or any movement behind him until something brushed against his

shoulder and told him he was not alone. Before he could react the voice came, its accents clipped and quiet.

"*Buenas noches, señor.*"

Without actually moving, Jeff felt as if he had jumped a foot and then the tension hit him solidly to hold him rigid and close his throat. It took a tremendous effort to break his paralysis but when his mind began to work there was nothing in it but hopelessness and despair.

So this is it, he thought. The long arm of *Segurnal* had caught up with him and he had been a fool to think he could long escape it. *So all right,* he thought. *You tried and you muffed it somehow so take your medicine.* He took a small breath and moved his head slowly, still not recognizing the voice until it came again.

"You're hot, Lane. You ought to watch it."

Jeff stared until the face at his shoulder swam into focus. Because his nerves were frayed his first reaction was one of anger rather than relief.

"Jesus, Webb!" he said and let his breath out in a long blast. "Is that your idea of humor? You scared hell out of me. Where were you?"

"In the doorway here. I saw you come but I thought I'd see what you had in mind. You gonna wait for Spencer?"

"Yes."

"Good enough. We'll wait together." He bent his head to examine his watch and slid a folded newspaper out from under his arm. "Take a look at this," he said. "We've got a little time. Take it up to the corner where there's some light. I'll stay here just in case."

Jeff took the paper, nerves quieting but still hesitant as he considered the suggestion. He did not understand the reason for it and he was reluctant to leave, yet something in Carl Webb's tone told him this was no idle whim. He glanced around, estimating the distance to the corner, took another look across the street, and started off, his legs stretching.

Light from a tiny soft-drink stand proved sufficient for his needs and he saw that he held a Spanish-language newspaper whose masthead proclaimed it: *Esfera*. It had been folded twice and when he turned it over his jaw dropped and his eyes popped with incredulity.

For what he saw was a one-column picture topping a one-column head. He could not read the head but the photograph was agonizingly familiar because it was his own. Having no idea where it came from, he stared at it a long moment, fascinated, despairing, and empty inside. When he realized what he was doing, he glanced up to see if anyone had noticed him; then wheeled, and hurried back into the temporary security of the darkness.

Carl Webb was standing just where Jeff had left him. He accepted the newspaper and put it back under his arm.

"Kind of knocked you over, Hunh?" he said. "I told you you were hot."

"What's it say?"

"My Spanish is weak, but I think it says you're wanted for questioning. Did you knock him off?"

It was not an accusation and carried no overtones. It was simply a routine question and he accepted Jeff's denial without comment.

"I had a session with the law this afternoon myself," he said, and related how he had gone to Grayson's office to find Karen Holmes already there and the body on the floor.

"What do the police think?"

"They're not saying," Webb replied. "I don't think they know."

"Where did they get my picture?"

"You had three of those tourist cards when you came, didn't you?"

"Sure."

"They had your picture on them, didn't they? And Immigration took two of them? Hell, it's simple; the trouble is you're not thinking. *Segurnal* knows when you got here. They borrow a photo from Immigration, make copies, and spread them around."

Silently Jeff agreed that the explanation was simple. What discouraged him now was the fact that *Segurnal* could work so swiftly and efficiently and, recalling things Cordovez had said, he began to wonder how long he could keep his freedom now that his picture had been published. To add to his dismay was the knowledge of that thirty-day term of arrest that was waiting for him if Pedro Vidal decided it was necessary.

"Why should they be looking for me at all?" he demanded querulously.

"I don't know," Webb said. "Why did you disappear?"

"I had a row with Grayson earlier," Jeff said, deciding that he had very little to lose in confiding in Webb. "I got a couple of scabs on my knuckles and a cut mouth," he said. "They're going to be hard to explain unless I can pick something out of the hat before I get grabbed."

He hesitated, considering Webb's background and his mission, and now his mind began to work and he put his thoughts in order.

"You didn't get your cash, hunh?"

"Not yet."

"Did you expect to?"

"What do you mean?"

"Did Grayson make you any promise?"

"Hell, yes. That's why I went to his office this afternoon. He told me this morning he'd have four hundred thousand bolivars—which is the same as a hundred and twenty grand and just as good—by four thirty. In five-hundred-bolivar bills," he said. "Eight packs of a hundred bills each. He said it would be all wrapped up and ready to go and I'm damn sure he wouldn't con me if he didn't think he could deliver."

Jeff agreed with the statement, though he did not say so. "And you think Spencer might have it?"

"I just want to be sure."

"You knew him in Las Vegas?"

"Sure I knew him."

"What kind of a guy is he? Could he have killed Baker or Grayson? Or both?"

"Dan Spencer," Webb said disdainfully, "is a mouse with the heart of a chicken. He hasn't the guts to kill anyone. He wouldn't even swing at you unless he was cornered and he's too fast on his feet for that."

"He had guts enough to blackmail Grayson."

"Who told you?" Webb demanded. "What kind of black-mail?"

Jeff spoke of the checkbook he had inspected and his theory of the reason for the payments.

"That could be," Webb admitted. "Grayson was running scared and Spencer knew all about the trouble. He's not the kind to get greedy about a big score so he tried a small tap; when it worked he was on the payroll."

"He was also around here this afternoon."

"Where?"

Jeff pointed up the street and explained how Spencer had come along with his invitation to have a beer.

"He could have seen somebody else besides me."

Webb thought it over a silent moment. A match scratched loudly and his squarish, muscular face was high-lighted as he put the flame to his cigarette. When darkness came again he said:

"If he did he won't be telling if there's a chance to col-lect. He's the kind of guy that fools around with things he can't handle and winds up dead."

"So how do you figure it?" Jeff said. "You're not standing around here for the fun of it."

"You know I'm not. . . . I'll tell you," he said after a moment's pause. "Have you ever been in the Westwind or any of those places in Vegas?"

"No."

"But you've been in gambling casinos where they play roulette."

"I've been in a couple."

"Well, in our place the drinks are free to gamblers. If you're having a play at the wheel or the dice game the drinks are on the house and you can generally find one at your elbow if you're not too busy to turn around. It keeps the gamblers happy and there's an angle, too, because a guy—or a dame either for that matter—with a few shots under his belt sometimes gets to thinking bigger than he should. If he's going well he gets more confidence and if it's the other way he gets the courage to forget the percentages and try to get even.

"It don't always work out for us because sometimes you run into a guy who is practically stiff—that kind gets real lucky sometimes—and he's on a streak and he hasn't got sense enough to drag down. I've watched guys like that who couldn't hardly see, guys you practically have to hold on the stool, stagger away from the table with a week's profits. But it don't happen often. Mostly the liquor works for us.

"But what I'm sayin' about Dan Spencer is this. He's a moocher. He used to hang around the gambling rooms and move in on some lush and watch his chance. When he thought he could get away with it he'd cop a couple of chips. He had it worked out so it was pretty hard to catch him but he'd been thrown out of half the joints in town and sometimes he'd get roughed up. Word got around. Finally the paper gave him the bounce and he drifted. I didn't know where he'd gone, or care, but what you say fits.

"Dan Spencer," he said, "is a scavenger. A hundred and twenty grand in cash is something he could smell a block and a half away. If he located it, and nobody was looking, and he thought he could get away with it, he'd grab it and run—if he didn't get scared to death thinking about it."

He grunted softly, a disdainful sound. "If you're trying to figure him for murder, forget it. But that money's around somewhere and I came a long way to collect. I may be grabbing at straws, but I'm going to go over Spencer's apartment like a vacuum cleaner and he's going to help. If you want to come you're invited."

He stopped abruptly, stiffened slightly, and dropped his cigarette. "Here he comes now," he said. "Let's go."

Jeff saw the thin, stooped silhouette as it passed the front windows of the newspaper office. He still was not positive, but Webb seemed to be, and now he was moving a step behind the man from Las Vegas, slanting diagonally across the pavement to intercept Dan Spencer.

Webb seemed to make no noise as he walked and Jeff, not knowing just what might develop, found himself moving on the balls of his feet. He sidestepped a man who was walking uphill and then Webb moved farther ahead so that he could come alongside Spencer from the inside of the walk. When he was close he spoke softly.

"Hi, Danny boy," he said. "Keep moving!"

Spencer's thin form seemed to straighten as he hesitated; then he was walking again, but slowly, as though he lacked the strength to put one foot in front of the other. Without turning his shoulders, his head came round first one way to look at Jeff, and then the other.

"Come on, boy," Webb said. "Your feet are dragging. Feel this thing in your back? Know what it is?"

"It—it's a gun. Take it easy, Carl," he pleaded, stuttering

now. He glanced round at Jeff and solicited his support. "Tell him to take it easy, Mr. Lane. . . . I don't know what this is all about," he said, a note of rising hysteria in his voice.

"See that doorway up ahead," Webb said. "That wide one. We'll stop there and I'll tell you what it's all about. I'm not going to start popping this thing in the street but I'd just as soon bend it over your head if you get noisy."

He reached out and pulled Spencer to a stop, half spinning him about. "This is fine," he said. "Do you know why I'm in town?"

"No," Spencer said, and then appealed again to Jeff. "What is this?"

"It's his idea," Jeff said. "He'll tell you."

"You're a liar, Danny," Webb said and poked the gun into Spencer's stomach hard enough to make him gasp. "You knew about Grayson's caper in Vegas. You knew we'd keep looking for him no matter how long it took. You run into him down here and put the bite on him— Don't argue with me, Danny," he said when Spencer started to protest. "This much we know. And I say you knew Grayson was going to pay off in cash so he could go home, one hundred and twenty grand worth."

"But jeez, Carl. You don't think—"

"Shut up!" Webb said, his voice still soft. "And don't look at Mr. Lane, Danny. He thinks probably you turned him in to the law this afternoon and he don't like you any better than I do. Where do you live?"

"I got an apartment—"

"How do we get there, walk or ride?"

"Ride, I guess."

"O. K., we'll get a cab. You can pay for it. O. K., Danny?"

"Sure, Carl. Sure."

"That's the way, Danny. Always play it safe."

15

THE APARTMENT house where Dan Spencer lived was somewhat larger than the building Julio Cordovez occupied but in the same sort of neighborhood and in the same section of the city. Paint was peeling from the walls of the foyer and there was an air of decay in the stuffy hallway as they started up the stairs and went along the second-floor corridor to a door near the rear.

Music with a Latin beat filtered into the hall from some near-by apartment and somewhere a child was crying. On the floor above, a door opened and the voices of a woman and a man rose in angry argument before the door slammed. Heavy footsteps thudded overhead to diminish briefly and then reappear as a man clumped down the stairs, swung round the landing, and continued on to the street.

"Come on, Danny," Webb said as Spencer fumbled with his key. "We haven't got all night."

Spencer muttered some reply and then the door swung open and he reached inside to snap on a light. Jeff, the last man in, closed the door behind him and looked about a squarish room that was cluttered, untidy, and depressing. The furniture had a third-hand look, the thin rug was spotted and dirty, and the windows in one wall were stained to a degree that suggested that, in daylight, they could be no more than translucent. Webb voiced the thought that was in Jeff's mind.

"Jesus!" he said. "What a dump."

"What do you expect?" Spencer said in injured tones. "Rents are high in this town."

"How much does it cost to keep clean?"

Spencer shifted his weight while Webb completed his survey of the room and Jeff noticed that the reporter looked neater than usual. His sallow face had a sullen expression but he wore a dark suit that was fairly well pressed and the white shirt and striped tie were an improvement over the open-necked sport shirts Jeff had noticed before.

"How many rooms you got, Danny?" Webb asked.

"There's a bedroom in there"—Spencer pointed to a small inner hall—"a bath, and a two-by-four kitchen."

"O. K., I'll start here. Sit down, Danny. You can watch."

"How about a drink first?"

"Not for me." Webb glanced at Jeff and winked. "You want something to settle your stomach?"

Jeff shook his head and eased down on a straight-backed chair near a table-desk whose edges had been charred into countless grooves by cigarettes which had burned too long unnoticed. Spencer sagged onto a couch with a frayed slipcover and the springs protested mildly under his weight.

Then Webb was moving slowly about the room, inspecting first the closet near the door, which proved to be a catchall for many things that cluttered the floor as well as the shelf above the hangers. This took about five minutes and when he faced the room again his hard-jawed face was glistening with perspiration. He took time to wipe it with the handkerchief in his breast pocket, sucked in a deep breath, and then came over to open the lone drawer of the table-desk.

He pawed through the papers, envelopes, and bills. He lifted the cracked fabric cover of the portable typewriter just to make sure no money was underneath. He lifted the cushions of the two easy-chairs, patting them thoroughly to make sure nothing was concealed. He pulled the curtains back from the windows, glanced behind them, opened the windows, and looked to see what was outside. The drawer of the occasional table yielded nothing and now he went over and told Spencer to get up. Spencer did so, the springs again signaling their presence.

Webb pulled the couch away from the wall, looked under it. He then gave it the same treatment he had given the easy-chair. Satisfied at last that there could be no other hiding place in this room he nodded to Spencer.

"Let's check the other rooms, Danny," he said.

"Go ahead."

"You can help. And anyway I want to keep an eye on you. You O. K., Lane?"

Jeff said he was fine and when the two moved out of sight he went over to the open windows. The fresh air felt good, but there was no view except the wall of the adjacent apartment house, six feet away, its windows darkened at this hour and mirroring only blackness. He got a cigarette going, hearing faintly the sounds of the search as drawers were opened and closed and furniture was moved; but now his mind was working and he knew there were still things he wanted to talk over with Spencer.

Webb remained something of an enigma. He had never known anyone quite like him. He could not be sure how much of his surface toughness and assurance was the result of training and experience and how much had been developed for window-dressing. He knew that Spencer had been scared, but this might have been due to the gun in his back. He also realized that Webb had been entrusted with an important mission and had come a long way to bring it off. But so far as murder was concerned he could not make Webb fit. If he had told the truth about the time of his arrival—and this was something the police could check—he could not have killed Harry Baker.

The murder of Grayson was less easy to rationalize because there was no way of knowing whether Grayson had been able to locate the missing cash. That Webb might beat him up if the money was not forthcoming was understandable, but not to the point of death. Webb was too smart to kill the source of income until or unless he had collected. And if he had collected why should he be wasting time with Dan Spencer?

He turned from the window as he heard the others come back, and he could tell from the expression on Webb's face that the search had been futile. Moisture glistened on his forehead and his brows were warped with frustration.

"O. K., Danny," he said finally. "You're clean here, but that doesn't mean I'm crossing you off my list. There could be other places and I have to keep trying. If you've got it, or if you find it and some of it sticks to your fingers, it's going to be too bad."

He hesitated, frowning now and his gaze thoughtful. "I might put out a little bonus if you can deliver. Say—five grand," he said, "and no questions asked. Five grand and your health, Danny. Because if I nail you with the bundle I'll take care of you another way."

He moved over to the door and looked at Jeff. "I'm taking the air," he said. "You coming?"

"I'll stick around awhile," Jeff said. "I've got a job to do myself."

"Yeah," Webb said. "I know what you mean." He took the folded newspaper from his jacket pocket, glanced once at the picture of Jeff, then tossed it on the couch. "Maybe you want to keep that," he said. "As a souvenir . . . See you," he said and went out.

The instant the door closed Spencer let his breath out in a long blast and his thin sallow face relaxed. He loosened the knot in his tie and unbuttoned the top button of his shirt. He wiped his glistening forehead with his sleeve, but the edges of his mouse-colored hair were dark with sweat, and traces of shock still lingered in the corners of his amber eyes.

"That guy scares me," he said finally.

"Maybe he was bluffing."

"Don't bet on it. I've seen that kind work before and brother, they can get mean. Once they get started on you they don't give a damn. They just don't care."

He sighed again as though such thoughts still bothered him, then turned and disappeared down the hall. A moment later Jeff heard water running and the clink of glasses, and presently Spencer returned, a bottle of whisky under one arm, two glasses in one hand, a pitcher of water in the other. He poured a quick drink and drank thirstily.

"Boy, did I need that," he said. "Go ahead, help yourself."

Jeff eyed the remaining glass. It had been rinsed, but it was obvious that it had been a long time since this particular glass had been subjected to soap and hot water. He did not want a drink, but he wanted to be sociable, so he splashed some whisky in the bottom, swished it around and added water. He took a sip and sat down on the couch.

"So you're the one who turned me in," he said.

"What?"

"You told the police you'd seen me this afternoon out in front of Grayson's office." He indicated his picture in the newspaper. "That put me on the front page. Maybe you told them my knuckles were skinned and my mouth was bleeding."

Spencer backed into an easy-chair, his expression sheepish. He stretched out his legs to reveal shoes that were scuffed and in need of a polish. When he leaned back his chest became more concave than ever.

"I didn't see your knuckles," he said. "You've got it wrong."

"Did you tell Ramon Zumeta you'd seen me?"

"Yeah, but—" He stopped and his Adam's apple jumped up and down in his throat. "That's not what put you in the jam," he said finally.

"What did? When did you know there'd been a murder?"

"When the law started cluttering up the street. Hell, you could hear them come. I ran out of the office and when I saw the mob I hotfooted it up there. I couldn't get in, but I saw Webb and that girl come out, so I tagged along down to *Segurnal.*

"With the city cops it would have been easy," he said by way of explanation. "They always co-operate with the press. They even got a room down at the headquarters building with a plainclothesman on duty to take the calls. Everything comes in, he types it up with carbons. Each paper's got a little box in a rack that's tacked to the wall. Somebody gets knifed, somebody gets banged up in a crash, somebody's taken to a hospital—you get a memo on it. That way the papers don't have to keep a man on duty like in the States. The police reporter just stops in there three or four times a day to see what's been happening and he follows up whatever he figures he needs. But *Segurnal* is different," he said and took another swallow of his highball.

"They don't give out that way. Lots of times they don't want any publicity. So I'm down there and I need a wedge to get in—hell, I have to get the best story I can, don't I?— and I send word in that I saw you outside Grayson's office."

"So Zumeta let you in."

"Sure, but it's not me that really put the finger on you."

Jeff stood up and removed his borrowed coat. He sat down again and got a cigarette going. He watched Spencer finish his drink and scratch the top of his chest before he leaned forward to fix a fresh highball. Jeff let the silence

build for another five seconds, his dark eyes brooding and
his lids half closed.

"All right," he said. "Who did?"

"The guy at the garage."

"What guy?"

"Maybe you don't remember, but when you walk up the
street you pass a plate-glass window, the only one in the
block. It's got some caskets in it."

Jeff nodded, remembering that this was true, and now
he also recalled the garage with its recessed ramp and
single gasoline pump.

"Next to that is this garage, and it just happens that
when you go by—it must have been when you went to see
Grayson—this guy is pumping gas for a customer. He's got
nothing else to do while the pump is working so he's looking round to see what's going on in the neighborhood."

He gestured with the glass. "Well, he sees you and he
notices you because you look American with your slacks
and white coat."

"Cord coat," Jeff said.

"To him it was white. He watches you go into Grayson's
doorway and that's all until Zumeta's men start combing
the block and questioning everybody to see if anybody's
noticed any strangers go into the building. This guy remembers you and by this time I've already said I offered
to buy you a beer so Zumeta gets in touch with Immigration and comes up with the photo on your tourist card. The
garage guy identifies you."

Jeff did not quarrel with the explanation. Coincidence
was something one had to accept in life, and it was coincidence in the form of Spencer and a man pumping gasoline at just the right time that had tipped the scales against
him. His own decision to postpone surrender as long as he
could had simply tightened the noose.

Now, studying the reporter and recalling the thumbnail

sketch Carl Webb had given of his character, he passed on
to the other thing that was in his mind.

"How long have you been collecting from Grayson?"

Spencer's eyes opened and for an instant it looked as if
he was going to deny the charge. Then, as though he no
longer had the will to argue this matter which he knew
to be true, he shrugged. He took up his pipe and blew
through the stem.

"About a year."

"You knew Grayson in Las Vegas."

"Sure, but I didn't know he'd been here awhile until I
ran into him at a meeting I was covering at the Tucan."
He paused and what he said then verified Webb's opinion.
It also gave Jeff a clear-cut mental picture not only of Spencer himself but of the way his mind worked.

"I looked him up the following week," he said. "Dropped
in at his office. I'd already done some checking and from
what I could learn he was doing O. K. He'd bought some
property that was getting more valuable every day, built
a nice house. He was representing some small Stateside
outfits and—"

"What about Fiske?"

"Fiske?" Spencer grinned and one corner of his mouth
dipped. "Dudley Fiske was a first-class errand boy. I think
the only reason he stayed was Diana Grayson—you've seen
her, haven't you?—or maybe he was just too tired to quit."

"All right," Jeff said. "So you saw Grayson. Then what?"

"I took it easy." Spencer inspected his drink, turning the
glass one way and then the other. "Out in Vegas he had a
reputation for being a mean bastard and I didn't want to
crowd him. I figured I'd better tiptoe around a bit, so after
we'd talked about this and that I said I could use some
extra dough and I had the time and maybe he could use
a publicity man.

"I said it might help his business if I got the right things in the paper. If he had some clippings to send back to the outfits he represented it might help. I said I could get his name in the paper at society things."

"And he bought it?"

"Not at first. He said no." Spencer looked at Jeff with one eye which drooped a little in a sly sort of way. "So I said that that was too bad. I said I just thought I'd ask and it was nice to talk to him again. I said I still had some friends in Vegas and the next time I wrote I'd tell them I'd seen him. I said they'd probably be interested to know how he was doing."

He hesitated again, unable now to resist a small secret grin. He gulped his highball and wiped his mouth.

"He got the message," he said. "At first I thought he was going to get rough about it—but what the hell, he knew the score. He never was a dope about things like that. He said maybe he could use a publicity man after all. He also made it clear what would happen if I got forgetful and wrote back to Vegas."

He chuckled as though a little proud of his cleverness. "I told him they weren't very good friends and I wasn't much at writing letters anyway."

Jeff sighed softly, feeling a grudging admiration for the man's technique and the native shrewdness that had prompted him to be modest in his demands.

"Three hundred B's a week," he said.

Spencer eyed him aslant. "How the hell did you know?"

"Does it matter?"

"No."

"Three hundred B's for not writing anything," Jeff said. "Ninety bucks a week."

"And I banked every dime of it," Spencer said, "because I've got this thing figured. I draw a pretty fair salary from the *Bulletin*. They have to pay it with living expenses like they are. And this is not a bad place. The climate's wonder-

ful—not most places where it's hotter'n hell and sticky too
—but here. Sun shines most of the time, not much rain,
and the altitude keeps it nice at night.

"So you work it out one of two ways," he said. "A guy
comes down here on a fat salary and he can figure on staying here or else he figures he'll only be here a few years
and then go home. If he likes it and stays he can live it up
—have a nice place, servants, join one of the clubs. Or he
can live quietly and hang onto his dough and to hell with
trying to keep up with the Joneses. He knows he's going
to get out and that when he does he can take his dough
back without the income-tax people grabbing half of it.

"That's me, brother." He tapped his chest. "Income tax
here is practically nothing. So I'm salting it away. When
I step off the plane, in New York, or wherever, I'll have a
nice stake and I won't have to worry about the tax people
until I start drawing a salary again. Why else do you think
I'd be living in a dump like this?" he demanded. "I could
do better, a lot better, but when I went back—and I will
some day—where would I be?"

He finished his drink but held onto the glass. He
slouched down another few inches and his head sagged.
His lips moved silently and he eyed the tips of his shoes
glumly.

"Now there'll be no more gravy," he said and grunted
softly. "No more publicity."

"You would have lost it anyway," Jeff reminded him.

"Hunh?"

"Grayson was paying off. He was going home."

He waited, aware that Spencer was watching him again
but because his head was still down his eyes were veiled.

"You knew Harry Baker and what he was doing," he
said. "I think you knew why he went to Barbados for Grayson and I think you knew Grayson had raised the equiva-

lent of one hundred and twenty thousand in cash for the payoff so he could go home."

"How would I know that?" Spencer asked sullenly.

"Because I think Grayson told you so. He was just the sort to rub it in when he could. He'd been trapped into paying out ninety bucks a week to you, and my guess is that when he knew he finally had you off his back, when he knew your little racket was about to collapse, he told you off. That sort of opportunity would give him a lot of pleasure and I doubt if he'd waste it."

When there was no reply, he said: "Furthermore I think you knew where the payoff was going to be. You were hanging around the Tucan that night—"

"Hanging, hell," Spencer said with some spirit. "It was an assignment. You think I'd take a chance on that kind of caper? With that kind of dough? You're crazy," he said. "I don't have that kind of nerve."

"So what are you going to do?"

Spencer put his glass aside and pulled himself erect in the chair. He gave the question four seconds of thought and then he glanced up, cocking his head to one side, his failure-shadowed eyes serious.

"I'm going to keep snooping."

"Doesn't that take nerve?"

"Not the way I do it." He tipped one hand. "I'm not greedy. I'm not kidding myself that I can find that cash, but I can try. A guy never knows when he might get a break. If I've got an angle I might go to Diana Grayson. She might pay—say, ten per cent—to get her hands on it. I'd settle for twelve G's and don't think I wouldn't. That way it would be a legitimate deal."

"And what about Carl Webb?"

Spencer opened his mouth and shut it, his expression indicating that this was something he would rather not think about.

"If you *did* locate that money," Jeff said, "and Webb heard you'd handed it over to Diana Grayson"—he paused to give the thought time to register, and decided to understate the situation—"I don't think he'd like it."

He stood up, his drink unfinished. He put on his jacket, not sure just what he had accomplished, but having a far better understanding of this man and the factors which influenced his thinking. Spencer did not bother to get up. His head had sagged again. It did not move as his eyes followed Jeff to the door, and they were brooding, reproachful eyes now, his look suggesting that it was Jeff who was responsible for his present unhappy state of mind.

Once again on the street and not knowing where he was, Jeff turned downhill because it was easier. He had to walk three blocks before he came to a main thoroughfare and located a taxi, and because he had learned the asking price was always high he tried a few words of his limited Spanish.

" *¿Cuánto?*"

"*Cinco* B's. Five B's," the driver added to indicate he recognized an American accent in spite of the suit.

"*Es mucho.*"

The driver shrugged. "*Cuatro,*" he said resignedly.

Jeff climbed in and brought out the piece of paper Julio Cordovez had given him. About to read off the address, he hesitated, prompted by some cautionary impulse that warned him again of the reputed long arm of *Segurnal.* Because he did not want to involve the little detective in the event the driver ever remembered this trip, he merely read the name of the street.

Five minutes later, when the driver made a turn and repeated the name, Jeff gestured for him to keep going. A block or so farther along he recognized Cordovez's apartment house, and he waited until they had gone another block before telling the driver to stop.

He tendered a silver five-bolivar piece and motioned the man to keep it. He waited until the cab started away before he started back downhill to the three-story building. The fact that the living-room light was on when he opened the apartment door did not concern him, because he expected to find Cordovez, and it was not until he stepped inside that he realized the corner chair was occupied by a woman.

She had sort of curled up there under a floor lamp, her legs tucked under her and her head back so the light fell on her face. She did not move in that first brief moment and Jeff stopped short, one hand still on the door as his glance focused. Only then was he sure that it was Karen Holmes who sat there watching him.

16

WHEN JEFF recovered from the first stunning impact of his surprise, he remembered that the door was still open and closed it behind him. He watched her support her weight on her elbows while she twisted her legs out from under her and got her feet on the floor. He saw her straighten her dress, and when she smiled excitement stirred in him and left his nerves atingle.

"Hello," she said. "I thought you'd never come."

Unable yet to voice his surprise, he could feel the grin stretching his face as this feeling of pride and pleasure expanded within him. Forgotten was the incident in Miami. For it seemed to him now that this was a girl he had known and liked for years. He did not yet understand how she had managed to get here; he only knew he was awfully glad to see her.

"For Pete's sake," he said finally. "How did you—"

"Julio brought me."

"Julio?"

"He came to the hotel. He said you wanted me to know where you were staying and I said I had to see you. I said there were some things I had to tell you. I bullied him," she said.

Jeff chuckled as he visualized the scene. "You must have."

"He couldn't cope with it. He wasn't very happy after we got here—maybe he was afraid his wife might come— but I promised to be a good girl and sit here in the corner until you came back." She paused and the smile went away. "Did you find out anything?"

He swung a chair over in front of her and sat down. "A little," he said and reluctantly brought his mind back to his problems. He told her first about Dan Spencer, the things he knew, the things that had been said.

"Did the police accept your story?" he asked as his thoughts moved on.

"About finding Grayson? Why—yes, I think so."

"What about Webb?"

"He told them he had a date, just like I did."

"Did he say why? Did he tell Zumeta about the hundred and twenty thousand?"

"Yes, but he had to explain it twice before Zumeta understood what he meant."

Jeff nodded, remembering that when he had last seen the *Segurnal* man, there had been no knowledge of either Webb or the money that Grayson had raised and was ready to deliver through Harry Baker.

"That'll give Zumeta something else to think about," he said. Then, his mind moving back, he again considered Diana Grayson and Dudley Fiske. He asked if either of them was questioned at headquarters.

"Both," Karen said.

"What did you think of them?"

"In what way?" she said, her incipient frown telling him he had not made his point clear.

He spoke of his first call at the Grayson house and the thoughts that had come to him then.

"That's an attractive woman," he said. "She looks and talks as if she had been brought up to expect the good things in life. She looks as if she might have been a lot of fun when she was younger, but she got a bad deal—with an alcoholic for a first husband, and she practically took Grayson on the rebound. The way I get it, he played up to her until he got his hands on what money she had. Since then it's been pretty grim for her."

He tried to explain his first impression of Fiske. "Until recently he'd been living with a myth. As a kid, he got the idea Grayson was the greatest guy in the world, and because Fiske never was a heavyweight, the disillusionment was a long time coming. He didn't want to let go of the idea he had created, because it was all he had left at the time. His one claim to importance was that he had been important to a man who had the importance he lacked. Or am I getting a little involved?"

"No." She shook her head. "I know exactly what you mean."

"He was selling printing—not too well, he says—and it was a great day when Grayson sent for him, a rejuvenation he was eager to have, a new start. Then, as time went on, the gloss wore off his idol. He saw what was happening to him and to Diana. Two unhappy people in the same house, bearing the same cross, understanding a mutual problem. I think, maybe without knowing it, they finally realized they were in love.

"Fiske was a different man this evening. I got the idea he had found some new strength and purpose, maybe through the woman. You could tell they were close to each other. She said they were going back to the States together, and I wondered—I mean, you're a woman and if you watched them down at *Segurnal* maybe you'd have some idea about how they felt toward each other."

"I think you're right." Karen moistened her lips and her eyes were a serious blue beneath the graceful brows. "He could hardly keep his eyes off her, and when she looked at him her glance seemed brighter. She seemed confident and assured and pleased with what she saw. It was the sort of look that women have when they are proud of a man and sure of his affection." She paused, her voice suddenly hushed. "Do you think Fiske—"

"I don't know," Jeff said, knowing what she meant. "But he could have, all right. It's a long lane etcetera, etcetera. They knew about the money and maybe old Dudley made up his mind he'd had too much from Grayson."

He tried to speculate beyond this but nothing came, and he saw that Karen had picked up her bag. When she opened it she brought out what looked like a gold thimble and offered it to him.

"This is why I came," she said. "I didn't tell the police I found it."

"What is it?" Jeff asked.

"I don't know. I thought you might."

She went on to tell how she had seen it under Grayson's desk and Jeff turned it over in his fingers, scowling intently and remembering the welts on his stepbrother's face. When a possibility occurred to him he voiced it.

"It could have come from a cane," he said quietly. "It seems a little small but—"

He stopped abruptly, head swiveling, as a soft knock came at the door. When he heard the sound of a key he was reassured, and a moment later Julio Cordovez slipped into the room and closed the door behind him.

"Ah-h," he said, his bright eyes assessing the situation in a glance. "All is well."

"So far," Jeff said. "Sit down and tell us what the police are doing."

"For one thing," Cordovez said, "they are looking for you. You were seen to enter the Grayson building this afternoon."

"Yeah," Jeff said and explained what he had learned from Carl Webb. He again displayed the two scabs on his knuckles. "And once they see these I'll be in it up to my neck."

"I agree," Cordovez said. "It is not a pleasant situation. We must arrive at some solution and quickly."

Jeff gave him the thimble, waited until the detective had a chance to inspect it and then explained where Karen had found it.

"What do you think?"

Cordovez took his time, his black eyes busy and his brows bunched. "You have a thought perhaps?"

"I think it might have come from the bottom of a cane."

"Considering the type of wound on Grayson's face I can agree to this."

"Who would have a cane?"

Again Cordovez took his time. When he spoke he corroborated the thought in Jeff's mind.

"Luis Miranda would have a cane," he said, his inflection suggesting he was not happy about the admission.

"What about the autopsy?"

"It has not been completed. The doctor will not say at this time whether he believes the wounds sufficient to cause death." He passed the thimble back to Jeff. "What do you propose to do?"

"I'm going to find out if this fits any of Miranda's canes."
Cordovez's brows climbed and doubt touched his glance.
"How will this be done?"

"I'll have to gamble that Mrs. Miranda may co-operate."

"Oh?"

"She was going away with my stepbrother," Jeff said.
"The airplane tickets prove that much. Furthermore I don't
think she was going just for the ride. She could scrape up
enough money for a ticket any time she wanted to. She
could have left before, but I don't think she wanted to give
up what she had until she found some sort of substitute."

He leaned forward and said: "We're not going to get
anywhere without making some assumptions, so I'm making one. I'm ready to assume that Muriel Miranda was in
love with my stepbrother, or thought she was, and either
way is good enough."

He digressed to explain how the woman had waited in
her car that morning. He spoke of her interest in the
amount of Grayson's stock inheritance and its potential
value.

"So if she was in love and ready to take what Grayson
could offer, she's going to be damned well crushed by his
death. With him gone she's still stuck with Miranda. She's
lost her man, and I have to go along with the idea that she
will want to get even with the one who killed him."

"Even if this is her husband?"

"All the more so, if she hates him. You don't have to be
very vindictive to want to punish the person who kills someone you love. It's a natural reaction. If I'm right I think
she'll be glad to co-operate, to do whatever she has to do
to punish the one who robbed her of her lover and her
future."

He was watching Karen as he finished, some part of his
mind recognizing again how lovely she was even as he
saw the somber glints in her dark-blue eyes. She nodded

her head slightly and a tiny frown marred the smoothness of her brow.

"Yes," she said. "I think you're right. I think I'd do the same. If she loved Grayson she has to hate the one who killed him. But I don't think you should try to talk to her."

"What?"

"I think I should."

Jeff leaned forward, understanding every word but not yet believing her.

"Oh, now, wait a minute."

"I mean it."

About to scoff, Jeff realized how very serious she was and checked the impulse.

"Why?"

"Because I can do that just as well as you can and with much less risk."

"Pardon me," Cordovez said.

Jeff looked at him.

"I believe the señorita is right."

"Thank you, Julio." Karen favored him with a quick bright smile and looked back at Jeff, her eyes challenging, her soft mouth determined. "I think I can tell better than you can if Mrs. Miranda was in love with Grayson. I'll find out if her husband has any canes. I'll bet I can make her show them to me. Why shouldn't I try?" she demanded. "It's not as if I was taking any great chance. I'll simply stop there in the morning after her husband has gone to the office and have a talk with her."

Jeff remained only partially convinced. He wanted to argue, but again he stopped. Not sure just why this girl should want to help him, he suddenly found a warm and satisfying glow in the knowledge that she felt that way.

"It is better," Cordovez said. "For you, daylight is bad except when absolutely necessary. Now that your photograph has appeared in the newspaper there will be too many eyes looking for you."

Before Jeff could reply, Karen had leaned forward and taken the thimble from his fingers. She replaced it in her bag. She gave him a saucy grin as she leaned back.

"After all I *am* a detective," she said. "Why shouldn't I work at it if I want to? I'm down here with expenses paid and I botched my assignment—"

"You didn't botch it," Jeff protested. "It wasn't your fault my stepbrother got himself killed."

"I made a lot of trouble for you in Miami and it didn't do a bit of good. If I hadn't done that, none of this might have happened. I'm not sure I can help but I'm certainly going to try."

She stood up and smoothed the dress over her trim hips. She touched her dark hair and her eyes still defied him.

"Also, in case you're interested," she added, "I'm turning in my card when I get home. I guess Dad was right. I'm not a very good detective and I've had about enough."

Cordovez rose along with Jeff and his dark glance was admiring as he inspected the girl.

"I will see that you get back to your hotel safely," he said. "Her suggestion is best," he said to Jeff. "I myself will see that no harm comes to her. You have my word." He touched Jeff's shoulder, his voice paternal.

"Do not wait for me. Go into the back room and close the door and go to bed. You need sleep. Tomorrow it will be better if you feel fit in case our luck turns and you have to face Ramon Zumeta."

Jeff argued no more. He glanced from one to the other and suddenly his worries seemed less burdensome as he realized for the first time how fortunate he was in having two friends such as these helping him.

17

IT WAS after nine when Jeff Lane waked the following morning, and because it was later than he thought, he jumped out of bed and stepped into the hall to see if Cordovez was still there. Certain now that he was alone, he came back to put on his borrowed trousers and shoes and then went into the bathroom to find the razor, towel, and brushless shaving cream that had been laid out for him.

When he came into the kitchen a note on the table said there was coffee on the stove which needed only to be heated, some fruit juice in the icebox. A paper napkin had been wrapped around a plate containing a sweet roll and butter, and the note invited him to use the eggs in the icebox if he desired.

He did not bother with the eggs, but he ate every crumb of the roll and drank two cups of coffee. He rinsed the dishes in hot water, and dried them, before he went back to the bedroom and completed his dressing. After that he began to prowl as the events of the night before came back to him and his nervousness increased. The few magazines in the living-room were in Spanish and when he sat down he found it impossible to remain there. He smoked his last cigarette and crumpled the pack and finally, unable to endure the uncertainty any longer, he telephoned Cordovez's office. He had some language difficulty with the girl who answered but he finally got across the idea that he wanted the detective to call his house.

By that time he had begun to worry about Karen Holmes,

but as there was nothing he could do about this he tried to assess the information he had gathered the previous day. The patterns his brain formed were in ever-changing combinations and the only thing he could be sure of was that it took him twenty-one paces to get from the far end of the living-room to the back of the inner hall. When the telephone finally shattered the stillness, he jumped for it.

"Where's Karen Holmes?" he demanded when Cordovez's familiar voice came to him.

"She is calling on Mrs. Miranda, as she promised."

"Alone?" Jeff said, shouting a little. "But you said you'd go with her."

"I tried," Cordovez said. "She would not permit it. She insisted that she take a taxi. She did not wish Mrs. Miranda to know that anyone was waiting for her."

"How long ago was that?"

"Perhaps a half-hour."

"Where are you?"

"Across the street from *Segurnal*. I am awaiting the doctor's report. I should not be long. . . . I think you worry needlessly, my friend," he said. "The señorita will come to you when she has finished. Be patient. I will telephone when I have news."

Jeff hung up and continued his pacing, his restlessness riding him even as he told himself that nothing could happen to Karen. There was another half-hour of this before he heard the knock, and when he opened the door and saw her standing there his relief left him momentarily speechless.

She was wearing a tailored yellow dress with black-and-white spectator pumps and the white handbag. Her cheeks were flushed, but the smile that came was weak and the dark-blue eyes seemed discouraged before she glanced away.

"Was it all right?" Jeff asked. "Did—you see her? There wasn't any trouble, was there?"

He heard her sigh as she flopped down on a chair and opened her bag. "I saw her," she said, and took out a package of cigarettes. When she fumbled as she tried to open it he reached down and tore off one corner. He offered her one and took one for himself. He furnished a light, still watching her, but no longer hopeful when he realized her eyes were evading him.

"Can I bum a couple?" he said, indicating the cigarettes.

"Take them," she said. "I can get more."

He sat down and watched her blow smoke toward the windows. He saw her breast rise and fall with another silent sigh. She took out the gold thimble which Jeff had hoped would turn out to be a ferrule and put it on his knee.

"I think you were right about one thing," she said finally. "I think she was in love with your stepbrother."

"What about the canes?"

"She said he had three that she knew of. She went and got them. They all had tips on them and anyway that one" —she pointed at his knee—"would have been too small around."

Jeff swallowed his disappointment and put the thimble into his pocket.

"Well, that's that," he said.

"I'm sorry."

"We'll think of something else." He paused, studying her and noting again the long lashes that framed her eyes. "What did you think of her? I mean, was she pretty upset? Did you get the idea she'd help if she could?"

"Yes. She didn't want to talk at first. I had to tell her about you."

"Maybe she thinks I did it."

"Not now, she doesn't. I could tell she'd been crying, but

there were no tears while I was there. She'd gone beyond that. Right now she's bitter and resentful. The one thing in her mind is to make whoever did it pay. She's in a pretty bad mood; it's hard to tell what she might do."

She thought a moment and said: "I could see it in her face. When she realized what I wanted she began to ask me questions. She kept at it."

"How much did you tell her?"

"Quite a lot. I thought I might as well."

"Did she know about the Las Vegas thing and the money?"

"Oh, yes."

"And she knows it's missing?"

"Yes."

"What did she say about her husband?"

"Very little. She didn't admit anything except that she knew her husband hated Grayson. From the impression I got I'm pretty sure she's considering the possibility that her husband was the one who killed him, but when I suggested it, she denied it."

"O. K."

Jeff put out his cigarette and stood up. He reached down and drew her from her chair, standing close to her now, his hands cupping both elbows. What he did then was as unexpected, even to him, as it was impulsive. Hardly realizing it, but attracted by some desire impossible to resist, he bent his head and kissed the soft mouth lightly.

When he drew back the dark-blue eyes were wide and a spot of color brushed each cheek but she did not say anything. She just looked at him. He could not tell how she felt and now he felt the hot blood in his cheeks and dropped his hands. He did not apologize, and in his confusion he tried to ignore the act by speaking quickly of other things.

"Off you go," he said. "You're through for the day. And thanks for everything, Karen. You're wonderful."

"But"—she drew back, the color still in her cheeks and her eyes suddenly concerned—"you can't just give up."

"I'm not giving up." Jeff said and grinned at her because he felt so good. "But you are. You're going back to the hotel and have a swim and a nice lunch and then you're going to take it easy."

He was moving her toward the door now, but before he could open it she resisted.

"I'm serious," he said. "What you really should do is get the first plane out of here."

She tipped her head. She gave him a tentative smile, but her concern still showed.

"And who's going to get the consul when you're arrested? Who's going to arrange for a lawyer?"

"I've already had an offer," he said, and told of Luis Miranda's threat.

She heard him out, but her young face stayed serious. "Please," she said. "If something doesn't happen, you will be arrested before long. Julio didn't say so, but I know that's what he's thinking."

"All right," Jeff said and opened the door. "We'll do something. He's working on a thing now," he lied. "As soon as I know something I'll call you," he said, and ushered her into the hall.

The knock that drummed on the door no more than five minutes later startled Jeff and he stood waiting until it came again. The threat of arrest that Karen had voiced was still with him, and the feeling had been growing in him that time was running out. No one could be lucky forever. When the knock came the third time he knew this could be it. With no way of guessing who might be outside, he suddenly realized he was tired of the apartment, tired of hiding; if this was a couple of boys from *Segurnal* he might as well get it over with.

This was what was in his mind as he stepped up and opened the door. Then he stepped quickly back, mouth gaping as he brought his stare to focus on the blond and ripely rounded figure of Muriel Miranda.

She was clad in a black silk suit with a short jacket and a snug-fitting skirt. Her straw-blond hair had a carelessly combed look, her tanned, broad-cheeked face was set and unsmiling. The eyes still looked as if they'd had their morning rinse in bluing but they seemed alert and purposeful as they gave him a quick inspection and slid beyond him to scan the room. When she stepped silently past him he voiced the first thing that entered his mind.

"How did you know I was here?"

"I followed your girl friend."

"But—"

"I decided if anyone knew where you'd been hiding, she would." She stopped in the center of the room and waited for him to close the door. "You sent her, didn't you? You thought Luis might have beaten your stepbrother with one of his canes, didn't you?"

"By the looks of his face, somebody had."

"Have you got that metal tip?"

Jeff took the golden thimble from his pocket and slipped it over the end of his little finger. She looked at it and then began to unbutton her jacket.

"I got to thinking after your girl left," she said. "There were only three canes, but Luis likes to ride, and I decided to do some more looking."

She pushed back the front of the jacket and now Jeff saw the leather loop hanging over the waistband of the skirt. While he stood there wondering what came next, she pulled her stomach in and elevated her chest. With the pressure eased on the skirt, she withdrew a plaited, alligator-leather riding crop. She tapped it lightly across her palm and thrust it at him, her blue gaze bright and intent.

"Try that for size," she said.

Jeff took the crop. It was heavier than it looked and as he tried to flex it he found it had the hard resiliency of a thin steel spring. When he slipped the ferrule over the end it fitted exactly.

He hefted it again before he put it on the table, the ferrule still in place, and now, recalling his impressions of Luis Miranda, he understood that this was a proper instrument for such a man to use.

"He knew you were planning to go away with Grayson," Jeff said.

"I guess he did."

"What changed your mind about your husband?"

She scowled at him. "How do you mean?"

"Sit down a minute," Jeff indicated a chair by the windows. He watched her hesitate and then accept his suggestion. "I know my stepbrother," he said. "And maybe a little about your husband. You'd been around when you married him, hadn't you? You were no shrinking violet. You must have either been in love with him or thought you had a good deal, or was it a little of both?"

She had taken a small gold case from her bag as he was speaking and now she put a cigarette in her mouth and held her face up for a light. When she had it she inhaled. She blew smoke at the ceiling and then she laughed, an abrupt sardonic sound.

"I'd been around all right," she said. "Ever since I got out of business school I've been standing on my own two feet. I started out as a sort of typist-secretary with a hotel. When I had some experience I did a lot of things. I've been a secretary, hostess, publicity woman, social director. I worked for hotels in New York, the White Mountains, Florida, Montauk. When they were getting the staff to-

gether for the Tamanaco it sounded like a good deal so I
came down.

"In the hotel business you see a lot of men. All kinds of
men with all kinds of ideas. I learned how to handle them,
how to get along with them, how to spot the different
types. I thought I'd seen about everything, until I met Luis
and changed my mind." She flicked ashes in the general
direction of a metal tray and considered the past a moment
before she continued.

"A girl gets tired of standing on her own two feet after
a while. Sure, I wanted to get married. I always intended
to. But with men around you all the time and plenty of
chances, you put it off. You want to be sure you're getting
something good for what you have to give. Well, Luis was
different. I didn't pay too much attention to him at first.
He was older and had grown children, but that didn't seem
important because he didn't look old, or act it.

"He was handsome, distinguished-looking. He came
from a fine family and I knew he had money, which isn't
something you readily do without. He was considerate and
polite and he was persistent. So"—she lifted one hand and
let it fall—"I fell for him. I was more in love with him than
I'd ever been before, and I knew something else, which to
a woman is important. He loved me; he still does. Probably
too much."

"He was jealous," Jeff prompted when she hesitated.

"God, yes! But it was more than that. They don't think
the way we do down here. Luis's idea of a wife was a
woman who stayed home and sat on her fanny when he
wasn't around. It didn't matter if I was bored stiff. It didn't
matter if I got fat or lazy or drank too much—just so I
stayed home. When we went to parties, and because of his
business that was fairly often, he was always at my elbow.
Like a leech. The minute I talked to some attractive guy
we had a threesome. It was awful. I told him so. Sometimes

I'd scream at him and I couldn't even get an argument out of him. It is the custom," she said, mimicking. "One must be proper. The wife of Luis Miranda must conform at all times.

"Well, I wasn't cut out for the hothouse treatment. I'd been around too much. What good is money when you can't have any fun with it? He had most of the servants bribed and until recently I couldn't even drive the car by myself. I was practically a prisoner, and if I could have got my hands on any money I would have left him long ago. But I made up my mind I wasn't going back to New York empty-handed. I never had any cash. I could charge what I needed. I might have managed the price of a plane ticket, but that wasn't enough. I figured I'd earned a lot more than that."

"Where'd you get the tan—Macuto?" Jeff asked, remembering the beach cottage Miranda had mentioned.

"Macuto? Hah!" She mashed out her cigarette and sat back, brow still furrowed and distance in her hard, fixed gaze. "I got it in the back yard. We got a pool with a high fence. I sit out there stripped down as much as I dare and bake."

"What about those?" Jeff pointed to the emerald solitaire, the platinum watch with the diamond-studded band, the diamond-and-aquamarine cocktail ring.

"The emerald is mine. The others belonged to his first wife. He loans them to me and keeps the rest locked up. He puts them out on consignment from week to week."

"If he kept you handcuffed the way you say he did, how did you manage those afternoons at Macuto with my stepbrother?"

That brought her eyes into focus. "How did you know?"

"Your husband told me."

She considered this a moment; then shrugged. "He didn't know about it at first. I suppose I raised such a fuss he decided to see what would happen if he let down the bars a little. He said I could drive my car without a chauffeur and go out afternoons by myself."

"By that time you already liked my stepbrother," Jeff said. "You were beginning to fall for his charming ways—or was it just the idea that he might be the answer to your problem of getting back to the States?"

"Maybe I was a little in love with him," she said. "But there was never any talk about my going away with him until that detective—"

"Harry Baker."

"—told him about the stock he was going to get if he went home."

"You knew about the Las Vegas thing?"

"Yes. Arnold told me everything."

"Not everything."

"What?"

Jeff took a breath and then, not quite knowing why he bothered, he spoke of the Arnold Grayson he had known as a boy, the trouble he had been in, the mean and vicious things he had done. He watched the blue eyes open as he spoke his mind but when he finished he knew she was not convinced that she had made a mistake.

"He wasn't that way with me," she said. "He admitted he had done some awful things, but he had changed— Men do change," she said defensively. "Women can help them. And anyway you don't love a man for what he was, but what he is."

"And you loved him?"

"Yes. I—" She hesitated and her lips trembled. She stilled them with an obvious effort and her chin came up. "I was willing to run away, wasn't I? I'm not a complete fool. Who can say in advance that a marriage will work out? I wanted to go with him. I wanted another chance, a new start."

She stood up abruptly, her lips compressed and her eyes

bleak. "If Luis killed him—" She left the thought unfinished but the implication had an ugly sound. "He did, didn't he?"

"I don't know," Jeff said. "They haven't even finished the autopsy."

"He wanted to kill Arnold," she said, as though she had not heard. "He would have done anything to stop him, not because he loved me, but because of that fanatical pride of his."

"But why should he kill Harry Baker?" Jeff said. "He didn't need the money, did he?"

"Need it?" she said, her voice harsh and metallic-sounding. "Of course not. But if he took the money, Arnold wouldn't dare go home. Don't you understand?"

Her look challenged him as the bitterness built inside her. "Luis knew about the money and why Arnold needed it. He knew a man was coming from Las Vegas to collect. He knew if Arnold couldn't pay he'd probably be killed. I think that's what Luis hoped would happen. Without that money to deliver Arnold would have to run, or hide. He was afraid. He had to pay, and unless he did he could not go back and neither could I."

She stopped, out of breath now, the prettiness twisted from her face. "I'll find out," she said. "Don't worry about that."

Jeff watched her jerk open the door, a little aghast at the fury of her words. He wanted to tell her to take it easy. He wanted to suggest that she tell the police what she knew. But before he could find the proper words, the door slammed and he was alone. Then, seeing again the riding crop and moving toward it, he was stopped by the jangle of the telephone.

"The autopsy has been completed," Cordovez announced in his quiet way. "Your stepbrother did not die as a result of the beating."

"Then what did kill him?"

"Asphyxia is the term the doctor used."

Jeff mouthed the word silently as he tried to define it. He understood that this would apply to a man who had inhaled gas. Would it also apply if a man had been strangled?

His thoughts hung there as his mind snapped back and he recalled the jacket that had been flung on the floor not far from Arnold Grayson's head as he lay dead on the office floor. Earlier, when Jeff had knocked him down, the coat had been draped over the back of a chair.

"You are still there?" Cordovez asked.

"I'm listening," Jeff said.

"There is one more detail."

"Yes."

"The nails of the first and second finger of the right hand were discolored. Scrapings taken from them were examined. These revealed blood and tissue and hair."

"Hair?" Jeff said. "Like from your head?"

"Much more tiny, and of a finer diameter. Such as might come from the back of a man's hand—or his wrist."

Jeff's mind considered this; then moved on. "See if you can find out about one more thing."

"I will try."

"There was a jacket on the floor by the body," Jeff said. "See if you can find out if there were any bloodstains on it."

"Very well," Cordovez replied. "And you will remain there until I come?"

"I'll be here."

Cordovez said that would be a good idea. He said he did not know how long he would be, but when he came he would bring sandwiches and beer.

18

KAREN HOLMES took Jeff's advice when she got back to the hotel shortly before noon. She felt hot and tired and discouraged and the swimming pool looked so inviting when she glanced down at it from her window that she peeled off her clothes and pulled on her suit. Taking her cap, a straw bag, and her key, she went down the back way, using the stairs.

Only a half-dozen of the web-seated aluminum chairs were in use, and when she'd been given two towels by the attendant, she selected a chaise which had been left adjusted in a flat position and deposited her things.

With the edges of her hair tucked up under her white cap, she dived from one side of the pool, stretching out the dive as long as she could and finding the water pleasantly refreshing after the first cool shock. She paddled about for five minutes and then stretched out on the chaise, face down. She reversed her position twenty minutes later when the hot sun began to spread its heat on her skin.

When she had taken her second dip and sat toweling herself she decided not to bother dressing for lunch, so she walked over to one of the round tables at the far end and caught the eye of one of the waitresses. She ordered a salad and iced tea, turning her back to the pool as she ate so she could look out over the distant rooftops of the city.

It was less easy to control her thoughts. She kept thinking of Jeff Lane and his trouble and her own part in the chain of events that had started in Boston. She was

ashamed of what she had been forced to do in Miami, but
her cheeks still tingled when she remembered his kiss and
the way he had looked at her. She did not believe he could
have done this if he had not forgiven her and this pleased
her greatly because she realized now how much his approval meant to her. She wanted so much to help him, and
because she did not know how, she went back to her room,
struggled out of the damp suit, and put on her robe.

She stretched out on the bed, intending only to rest a
bit, but she made the mistake of closing her eyes and once
her thoughts began to drift she was asleep. It was after
three when she awoke and now, realizing what had happened, she twisted off the bed, annoyed with herself for
wasting this time.

Although she had no particular place to go, she showered hurriedly and then dressed, selecting a checked skirt,
a tailored blouse, and the white blazer. When she had in-
ventoried her bag and her wallet, she went downstairs
and took the first taxi in the line, telling the driver to take
her to the avenida Urdaneta. She had no particular destination in mind, but she had seen the modern shops along
the street near the old center of the city, and it was her
intention to do some shopping once she was in the right
neighborhood.

The corner she selected held no special significance as
she stepped out of the cab and paid the driver; but as she
stood waiting for the light to change, it seemed familiar.
When she glanced up at the street sign she knew why. For
this was the cross street where Arnold Grayson had his
office. If she turned right, here, and walked two blocks,
she would come to it, and now, moved by some unaccount-
able impulse, she found herself making the turn and starting up the sloping street.

She was thinking now and took no notice of the pedestrians she passed. She still had no purpose but seemed moved

by some fascination that drew her back to the scene of the
crime. She had made the same trip the previous afternoon,
riding, that time, and taking with her the hope that she
might get the stock assignment she had been sent here for.

That was all over now. A man was dead—two men—and
Jeff was hiding. So far she had been unable to help him.
She saw no hope of helping now, but still she continued
on until she passed the open door of the *Daily Bulletin*.
Up ahead was the gray masonry building she knew so
well, but suddenly, her thoughts flying off on some illogical
tangent, she found herself wondering about Dan Spencer.

She did not know why, but having once made the reporter the center of her attention, her mind went on and
things began to happen. Her footsteps slowed. She stopped
and glanced back over her shoulder. Because of the narrow
walk, people had to detour about her or step into the street
and so she crossed to the opposite side and turned to
inspect the entrance of the newspaper office.

Spencer had been one of those who had seen Jeff outside
Grayson's office. He worked in the neighborhood. He had
also been at the Tucan the night Harry Baker had been
murdered.

Was this coincidence?

There was no answer to this, but she could not get the
thought out of her mind. She began to recall the things she
had heard about Spencer, the things Jeff had said the night
before about Spencer and Carl Webb and the money.

So far no one suspected him of murder. He had been
around when things happened but he had never been a
suspect. Why not, if he knew about the money?

His office was less than a half a block away. Suppose he
had somehow managed to get his hands on that money
yesterday afternoon? How simple it would be to explain
his presence, to take the package—or whatever it was—and

stroll back to his office and put it in the bottom of a desk drawer.

Had anyone thought of that?

His apartment had been searched—but what about the office? *Oh, stop it!* she thought, as her mind raced on uninhibited.

But it was not that easy. Once having started, she kept building on her imaginative premise until she had nearly reached the point of doing something about it. She wondered if Spencer would be working at this hour. She could easily find out, and if he was, what harm could there be in going in and talking to him? She could think of some excuse and maybe she could find out something that would help.

This is what she told herself, as she stood there drawing on her reservoir of nerves. Then, when she was at the point of acting, the decision was made for her and she got the break she had been hoping for.

Some intuitive impulse which could never be explained had put her in the proper spot at the proper time. But it was luck, or fate, or chance—the name did not matter—that gave her the chance to pursue her project. For even as she stood there, still undecided, Dan Spencer walked out of the doorway she was watching and turned downhill.

He looked better groomed than usual with his dark suit and necktie, but it was the envelope he carried under one arm that sent the quick excitement coursing through her veins and gave the green light to her imagination. And now, already conditioned by suspicion and uncertainty, she gave in to the following impulse without further thought.

She was walking now, trying to keep pace with Spencer's stooped, loose-gaited strides. The questions that popped into her mind she answered as best she could. She knew, first, that the Manila envelope was at least ten inches by twelve. From a distance she thought it had a sizable bulge, but she could not be sure.

And she knew that money could be carried in such an envelope, a lot of money, if the bills were in the right denominations.

And who knew how big the bills were? Had anyone said? How much room would one hundred and twenty thousand dollars take up? How much if the money was in bolivar bills?

She realized now she did not care. For all she knew Spencer had an envelope full of copy paper and was on his way to some interview. It did not matter. She intended to find out where he was going, and if her thoughts and actions proved to be ridiculous, she could laugh about them later.

She stopped suddenly when she saw him come to Urdaneta and wait for the traffic light. Keeping to the inside of the walk and not wanting to miss the light herself, she advanced slowly. She crossed the street safely, still a third of a block behind the thin figure. At the next intersection he crossed to her side and she had to stop again.

Halfway down the next block he seemed to vanish, and she felt a momentary thrust of panic. She hurried forward and then, uncertainly, she slowed her steps until she saw the familiar sign of a well-known airline above a plate-glass window. Then, even before she peeked round the corner of that window, her pulse quieted as she wondered if Spencer's business might have to do with a flight reservation.

Dark-haired men passed by and eyed her with approval. Some hesitated hopefully and most of them smiled. She ignored them all, not worrying about appearances now as she sneaked a quick look from the edge of the window.

A glance was enough to tell her that Spencer had

stopped at the counter at the far end of the room. It was a
sizable office, with several pillars, some leather settees and
chairs, and a stand-up desk along the wall. Spencer stood
with his back to the entrance, his elbows propped on the
counter, as a clerk began to fill out some form on a typewriter. Other men and women were similarly occupied
and still others waited on the settees. In all, there were
twenty or more people in the room, and when Karen saw
the telephone booth near the door she knew what she had
to do.

One eye on Spencer's back, she moved quickly through
the glass doors and slipped into the telephone booth. She
closed the door, feeling secure now as she opened her bag
and looked for Julio Cordovez's telephone number. She
no longer had to watch Spencer. Whatever happened at
the counter she could find out later. All she had to do was
wait until she saw him leave the office.

Her voice trembled a little with excitement when Cordovez answered and she identified herself and asked for
Jeff.

"Jeff," she said a moment later and then the excitement
got the best of her and she started to babble. "I think I
might have something. It's Spencer. He's in a downtown
airline office. I think he's making a reservation and—"

"Karen!"

The quick and forceful sound of his voice stopped her
and told her she'd been letting her emotions run away from
her. She heard him ask where she was. She told him.

"And what's this about Spencer?"

"I followed him here. I saw him come out of the newspaper office and he had this envelope under his arm and
I—I followed him."

"Why? What were you doing there in the first place?"

The question stumped her for a second because it was
so hard to answer. Why had she gone there? Could she

explain an impulse or justify by logical means an intuitive compulsion she herself did not understand? The answer was no, and suddenly she was annoyed with his questions and impatient with his attitude.

"What difference does it make?" she cried. "He has an envelope, too, a large one. It might even have the money in it."

"All right," Jeff said. "All right. Slow down. You followed Spencer. He's at the ticket counter. Now where are you?"

"In a phone booth near the door. I'm going to wait right here until he leaves and then I'm going to the counter and find out if he actually has made a reservation."

She hesitated and when there was no reply she said: "Jeff!"

"I'm thinking," he said. "Maybe you've got something. Just be sure he's gone before you go to the counter. And don't try to follow him, do you hear?"

"All right."

"Let him go. Don't fool with him. Promise?"

"I promise."

"Good girl. After you've checked at the counter call me back and we'll figure out what to do next. O. K.?"

She broke the connection but kept the telephone to her ear in case anyone should look through the door and wonder what she was doing. She put on her dark glasses and turned her head so that she could get an oblique, corner-of-the-eye look at the entrance. She sat that way, with the stuffiness increasing and the perspiration prickling on her body, until Spencer cut across her line of vision. She counted five very slowly before she replaced the instrument and opened the door; then she hurried to the counter, waiting until she could get the same clerk who had talked to Spencer.

"Did Mr. Spencer get his reservation?" she asked.

"Mr. Spencer?"

"The tall, thin man who was just here."

"Oh, yes. Yes, we had a seat for him."

"On the nine o'clock flight?" she said, pulling the figure out of the air.

"Not nine," the clerk said. "Ten. Twenty-two hundred hours. That's the direct flight to New York."

"Oh." She gave him her best smile. "Well, thank you very much."

She turned away, the excitement churning in her now as she digested the information. When she came to the telephone booth she did not hesitate. She had promised not to follow Spencer and she was keeping that promise, but she was much too pleased with herself to give her information over the telephone. It would take no more than ten minutes to get to Cordovez's apartment, and this was a message she wanted to deliver in person. She wanted to see Jeff's face when she told him; she wanted to know just what he intended to do.

She went through the door to the street and turned uphill, walking quickly, oblivious of her surroundings. She had taken perhaps five steps when something hard and round pressed suddenly against her side. Before she could react she heard the voice in her ear.

"If you want to stay alive keep walking, sister!"

Shock kept her moving in that first instant when her spine stiffened and her throat closed. She could not think, she could not even breathe; she only knew that somehow she kept moving as the voice went on.

"Don't open your mouth and don't look round. Just walk nice and easy!"

She moved like an automaton, propelled by fear now and waiting for the next command.

"See that yellow cab across the street? That's where we're going. You're doing fine. Stay with it. When we get in the cab sit still. Let me do the talking and you'll be O. K."

The horrible pressure in her side stayed with her as they crossed the street against the traffic. The taxi driver saw them coming and reached back to open the door. Not until she slid over on the seat did she actually identify the man who threatened her.

19

JEFF LANE had taken the telephone call at five minutes after four and by four fifteen he had started to sweat. He had his jacket off, his shirt was unbuttoned at the throat, and when he ran his fingers through his hair they came away damp.

"Why doesn't she call?" he demanded, turning on Cordovez, who sat by the window.

The detective shrugged and his voice was placating. "It is only ten minutes, my friend. It is no good to worry so soon."

Jeff resumed his pacing and the minutes dragged by on leaden feet. Every now and then he would repeat his question, his tone more savage as the seeds of panic began to sprout inside him. By four thirty even Cordovez's smooth face began to show concern and now, his mind made up, Jeff could stand it no longer. He buttoned his shirt and reached for his jacket.

"Come on," he said.

"But where?"

"How the hell do I know? Something must have happened to her. We can try the airline office, can't we? We can check on Spencer."

"She promised she would not try to follow him."

"So maybe she broke her promise."

"Wait." Cordovez put up his hand. "There may have been some misunderstanding. Let me try the hotel first."

He dialęd and spoke briefly. After another half-minute he spoke again and then covered the mouthpiece with his palm.

"She is not in her room. I am having her paged." Still another minute dragged by and finally he muttered something else and hung up. "She is not there."

He studied Jeff a moment, understanding his frame of mind but thinking of more practical matters.

"Let me go look," he said. "I do not think it is wise—"

"Nuts," Jeff said. "I'm not worried about *Segurnal.* We've got enough now to get me clear if they pick me up. It's Karen I'm worried about, don't you understand?"

"Of course. That is what I meant. I think someone should stay in case she telephones or comes here herself."

The logic of such reasoning steadied Jeff when he recognized the wisdom of the words. Someone should stay here, at least for a while, and Cordovez, a native of the city, could do the outside work more efficiently. It was hard to face the prospect of waiting alone, but in the end Jeff gave in.

"All right," he said. "Try the ticket office first. Then go to Spencer's place. If you don't find anything try his office. After that come back here and pick me up. If Karen hasn't shown by then she won't be coming here at all."

"It is best that way." Cordovez stepped to the door. "I know the waiting will be difficult for you, but it must be done. I will be back as soon as possible. Have faith, my friend."

It was five thirty when Julio Cordovez returned, and

one look at his somber face told Jeff the news was bad.
"What happened?" he said.

"She was not at the ticket office, so I went to Spencer's
apartment and let myself in. It was empty."

"Did you find anything to give you the idea she *might*
have been there?"

"Nothing." Cordovez turned away, his disappointment
showing in his voice. "I went to the offices of the *Bulletin*.
They told me Spencer had been in this afternoon but they
could not say when he would return. They thought perhaps
around seven. But one thing I learned," he said grimly.

"What?"

"At the airline office I made other inquiries. Spencer has
a seat on the ten o'clock flight to New York."

Jeff thought it over, eyes narrowing and the tension still
warping his mouth. The discovery suggested many possibilities but at the moment did little to allay his fears for
the girl.

"O. K.," he said. "We can stop that if we have to, but
that's damn near five hours from now. Where is she?" he
asked hoarsely. "She didn't just disappear. She's got to be
some place."

He hesitated, making another effort to get his thoughts
in order.

"She must have found out something," he said. "She must
have run across some evidence that hooks up with murder.
Somebody found it out and grabbed her. It's got to be that
way. If it's not Spencer then it's got to be Fiske, or Diana
Grayson, or Luis Miranda. They're the only ones involved."

He took a breath and this time when he reached for his
coat he put it on. He was no longer worried about
Segurnal. The only important thing was Karen Holmes and
he was sick of inaction, sick of having people do things
for him while he did nothing for himself.

"Let's go, Julio," he said. "And don't give me any argument. If she's being held at Grayson's or Miranda's we'll damn soon know it."

He opened the door and started down the hall, Cordovez at his heels. When they got into the sedan he thought of something else and mentioned it.

"What about Carl Webb?"

Cordovez considered the suggestion, but when he replied he did not sound convinced.

"It is a possibility."

"That's all we can hope for," Jeff said. "If he got his hands on that dough and Karen happened to find out about it—"

He did not have to complete the thought and Cordovez interrupted. "It will be a simple matter to check his room and it will not take long."

They drove in silence after that and when they approached the Tucan, Cordovez parked some distance from the entrance. "I will have a look," he said. "Please stay here."

Jeff did not argue this time, but lit a cigarette and watched the little man hurry away. He watched until Cordovez disappeared through the front entrance and then sat that way, fighting his anxiety and keeping his impatience in hand until Cordovez came hurrying back to the car.

"The room is empty," he said as he stepped on the starter. "Those at the desk do not recall seeing him recently. . . . You wish to go to Grayson's first, or to the Miranda home?"

"Which is closer?"

"There is little difference."

"Then let's try Grayson's."

Diana Grayson eyed her visitors with some surprise, but her company manners were excellent. She invited them in and listened politely to what Jeff had to say. Then she shook her head.

"Why no," she said. "I haven't seen Miss Holmes since the other morning."

Jeff's glance had been inspecting the room and the lawn and the hallway as she spoke, and then, because he knew how easy it would be to lie about such a thing, he said:

"Do you mind if we look around?"

He watched the brows arch and the quick resentment flicker in her eyes. He thought she was going to refuse, but she laughed and spread one hand, palm up.

"Help yourself," she said coldly. "You don't mind if I pass up the tour, do you?"

Jeff was in no mood to resent the snub and when she sat down on the divan and opened a magazine, he started off, not sure where he was going but determined to inspect every room and every closet. With Cordovez's help it did not take long. The maid in the kitchen gave them no more than a curious glance, but Cordovez stopped long enough to converse with her briefly.

He caught up with Jeff in the first bedroom, checked the bath, went on to the second bedroom and bath. A corridor which angled from the main hall led down two steps to the small wing which Dudley Fiske occupied, a large bedroom complete with television, a bath, and a separate entrance.

Certain now that no one was concealed here, Jeff led the way out the door and continued on to the garage. A late-model hardtop occupied one half of the space, but there was nothing else, and now he went back to the house and asked about Dudley Fiske.

"He went out to get some liquor." Diana Grayson smiled at Jeff and her sarcasm was softly cadenced. "He should be back any minute if you'd care to wait."

When Jeff hesitated, Cordovez touched his arm and a jerk of his head conveyed the idea that it was time to leave. When they went back to the car, he explained why.

"I spoke to the maid," he said. "The girl has not been here." He drove down the hill and turned into an avenue which took them toward the Caracas Country Club. "Also," he said, "I took time at the Tucan to telephone Miranda's office. He has not been there since noon."

He drove silently then until he came to a district where houses became more expensive-looking and the surrounding lawns were wider. Mostly the architecture was traditional rather than modern and as they approached an impressive white-stucco house on the right, he stopped the car.

"Permit me to make a suggestion," he said. "I share your anxiety for Miss Holmes, but I think it would be wise to use caution here."

Jeff looked at him, not understanding what he meant and, in his particular frame of mind, not exactly caring. He had had enough of caution. What he wanted was action and he said so.

"I understand," Cordovez said. "Still I do not think it will be easy to search this house if Luis Miranda is home. In fact he will not permit it. As a matter of pride he would resist. Also, there is a simpler way to get the information you desire."

"Name it."

"I will go to the rear and speak to the servants. They have respect for authority. When they see I am a detective they will tell me what I want to know. Believe me, the girl could not be in this house without their knowledge."

Sentenced again to inaction because he could not argue with such commendable reasoning, Jeff stayed in the car. He saw the little man edge round the corner post of the driveway gate and disappear into the dusk which had been moving down the surrounding hillsides. Once, he looked at his watch. Ten minutes of seven. And if Karen was not here, where was she? What could he do next?

Five minutes passed, and somewhere in the distance a bell tolled softly. The darkness came swiftly then and it was darkest of all in his heart because it seemed now that this was his fault. If he had given himself up and told his story yesterday afternoon this could never have happened; there would have been no need for Karen's help, no reason for her to take chances.

Again he glanced at his watch while the torment grew inside his head and he tried to think, to remember details, to look ahead and decide what could be done next. From out of the vortex of those thoughts he recalled the riding crop and the metal ferrule and now, focusing for that instant on Luis Miranda, he understood that there could still be one more place the girl might have been taken. It would be a remote chance, but the possibility existed, and possibilities were all he had left.

Cordovez opened the car door before Jeff knew he was there. "She has not been there," he said. "Nor has Luis Miranda. He left this morning and has not yet returned."

"All right," Jeff said. "Let's travel. Do you know Macuto?"

"Of course."

"Miranda has a beach cottage there. Do you know where it is? Could you find it in the dark?"

"I think so." Cordovez got the car under way and leaned back. When he spoke there was a note of incredulity in his voice. "You believe it is possible—"

"I don't believe anything any more," Jeff cut in. "But we have to go to the airport, don't we? And Macuto's out in that direction, isn't it?"

"Yes. The next little town to La Guaira."

"So let's have a look."

"It can do no harm," Cordovez said and settled down
to the job of driving.

20

JEFF LANE remembered very little of the ride to Macuto.
Because he was afraid to hope too much he tried not to
think at all and stared sightlessly out the windshield as
they sped along the toll road to the coast.

The lights at Maiquetia roused him and he heard the
thunder of some plane on its take-off run. Then they were
going along the waterfront at La Guaira with its stores on
one side and the docks on the other. A cruise ship, every
porthole alight, lay alongside a modern warehouse, and
the dimly lit hulks of two freighters stood silhouetted
against the sky. Then the lights were gone again and they
went along quiet, tree-lined streets, sometimes following
the coast and sometimes farther inland.

The sea was always on his left and presently they were
cutting through a narrow plain. Here and there he could
see an apartment house, while on the right pale blurs on
the landscape spoke of sand traps and a golf course. Jeff
spoke of this and Cordovez nodded.

"Caraballeda Yacht and Golf Club," he said. "Soon we
will be there."

Luis Miranda's beach house sat on a slope which faced
the sea, its veranda suspended on cantilevers and the rear
half snug against the ground. Its design was modern and
its light color made the outlines distinct, but to Jeff it had

only an empty look that served to depress still more his already flagging spirit.

A drive led to a basement garage. As he followed Cordovez over the traprock surface he offered a silent prayer; for he had run out of ideas and there was nothing left for him to do. He repeated it as the beam of the detective's flashlight sprayed the drive and then he stopped as Cordovez bent down to examine the surface more closely.

"A car may have been here recently," he said and then cut across the grassy slope to a door protected by a metal grill.

Another look with the light showed this to be chain-locked, and now they continued along the front and up the grassy slope toward the rear. Two of the windows on this side could be reached from the ground. Both had similar metal grills to guard the glass, but when Cordovez examined the second one with his flash he whistled softly and the oath that followed was tinged with excitement.

"This one has been forced," he said. "The catch is broken."

And then he was fumbling with the grill, prying at it, forcing it wide on its hinges. The light went out, but Jeff heard the window being raised and now he was crowding close, giving the little man the boost he needed, and climbing in after him.

The room they stood in proved to be a kitchen. Jeff moved ahead into a hall and called out. "Karen!" he said, and held his breath as the word bounced off the walls.

"Let me," Cordovez said, pushing past him. "I have the light."

He hurried on, heels clicking hollowly on the tile floor. He opened the door on his right and sprayed light into the room. Then he seemed to recoil, inhaling through his mouth with a hissing sound.

Before he could speak, Jeff was staring over his shoulder,

seeing the figure in the white blazer spread-eagled on the bed, the dark hair on the pillow, the towel which had been tied over the mouth. When he saw the eyelids blink against the light, his relief overwhelmed him and it was Cordovez who reached the side of the bed first.

With the flashlight on the floor he began to untie one of the towels that had fastened an ankle to a bedpost and now Jeff was bending over her. He slipped the makeshift gag down over her chin and swallowed hard to clear his throat. He saw the lips move and recognition touch the wide-open eyes.

"It's O. K., baby," he said thickly. "It's all right. We'll have these things off in a minute."

He tugged at the towel which held a wrist extended toward one head-post and turned immediately to the other. By that time Cordovez had freed the ankles and now, as she tried to sit up, Jeff slid an arm under her shoulder and lifted her to a sitting position as her feet swung to the floor. He sat down beside her, still with his arm about her, and now he could feel her body shudder and the rib cage expand as she took a great tortured breath. When she tried to speak the sound that came forth was no more than a whisper and he touched his finger gently to her lips.

"Easy," he said. "Don't try to talk yet. . . . Julio, see if you can find some water."

Julio hurried off and the light went with him. Gradually Jeff could feel her body relax and her breathing become regular. Her head was on his shoulder now and he sat very still, until reaction set in and his hand began to tremble. He did not know what to say or how to explain his gratitude and relief and finally he chuckled and kept his voice light.

"I seem to be the one that's shaking," he said and let his arm relax. "Julio!"

"Coming."

Then the light glowed in the hall and Julio came scurrying in holding a glass which had a light-brown tint.

"There is a little brandy with the water," he said. "Just a little. It will be good for you."

Karen accepted the glass and whispered her thanks. She took a small sip and then another. She moistened her lips, flexing them slightly, and then she took a big swallow and sighed.

"Yes," she said. "I needed that very much."

Jeff told her to drink some more and when she had complied he could contain his curiosity no longer.

"Was it Miranda?" he asked.

"Miranda?" She looked at him and blinked. "Oh, no. Spencer."

Jeff glanced at Cordovez. It took him a long moment to accept the statement and then, perhaps because he could not so easily throw off the nervous tension which had for so long held him in its grip, he felt strangely annoyed and spoke sharply.

"I told you not to follow him," he said. "You promised."

"I didn't."

"You said you'd phone."

"I was going to but"—she paused to look down at the glass and her tone was apologetic—"I—I wanted to tell you myself. I didn't know he had seen me. I was going to get a cab and drive right out to the apartment. I came out of the office and started up the street and Spencer came up alongside me—I didn't know who it was then—and put what felt like a gun in my side."

She went on hurriedly to explain what had happened and when she ran out of breath she took another and said, her tone rueful:

"It wasn't even a gun. It was a pipe."

"Where did he take you?"

"To his place. He locked me in a closet and I heard him talking on the telephone and pretty soon a man came. I don't know who he was but he was big and he had a hard, twisted face. He scared me. They brought me out here. Spencer did not believe anyone would think to look for me here and—"

Jeff swore softly as rage kindled inside him. "We'll take care of Spencer."

"He didn't hurt me. He said he was sorry but he had to do it."

"He tied you up," Jeff said hotly. "You might have been here for days."

"No," she protested. "Really. He said he would mail an anonymous letter to Ramon Zumeta telling him where to find me. He said I'd have to stay here tonight but the police would come in the morning to release me. By that time he would be in New York."

"Not now, he won't," Jeff said.

"Yes," Cordovez said. "It is time to go, I think. It is better if we are waiting at Maiquetia when Spencer arrives."

Cordovez explained the procedure when they drew up at the edge of the well-lighted plaza in front of the terminal building.

"We will park here and watch," he said as he stepped from the car. "He will probably come in a taxi, which will stop somewhere in this area. It will be good if we can take him before he can reach the building." He opened his coat and his hand slipped inside, and though Jeff could not see it, he knew there was a gun tucked away somewhere. "If you will permit it," Cordovez added, "I think I can handle this myself."

"To hell with that," Jeff said.

"Pardon."

"You take care of the taxi driver. If you talk fast you can keep him quiet. Spencer is mine."

He felt the girl's hand on his arm. "Maybe Julio's right," she said.

"I don't care if he's right or not," Jeff said. "This time old Jeff gets into the act."

He moved up alongside Cordovez and as he did so the detective hissed softly and lifted one hand.

"I think he has arrived," he said, pointing to a taxi that had stopped about fifty feet away. "Yes. Come," he said and started moving fast.

Jeff stayed with him, seeing the driver step down and start for the trunk at the rear. On the opposite side, in the shadows, a man alighted and Jeff veered that way. For an instant the lights bothered him and then he was safely past them, certain now that the man was Dan Spencer. He had a blue flight bag in one hand and as he started to turn toward the rear where the driver was unlocking the trunk, Jeff called to him.

"Hey, Spence!"

The man wheeled, head slightly bent as he peered through the darkness. Jeff was still fifteen feet away but moving fast and now, as Spencer's hand whipped back under his coattail, he closed with a rush.

He saw the hand come round, the metallic gleam of reflected light on a gun barrel but by that time he was close enough and he moved with confidence. This was what he wanted. This was what he had been waiting for. He grunted happily as he grabbed the gun barrel before it leveled off.

He heard Spencer's muffled curse, heard the flight bag drop as the reporter swung at him. After that it was no contest. For Spencer was a powder-puff. Six feet tall and ill-conditioned, he would have weighed no more than a hundred and forty in a winter suit, and when Jeff, in close now, hooked his right against the bony chin, that was it.

The gun came free in his hand as Spencer sagged against him. Jeff held him that way, pocketing the gun and then reaching for the flight bag. When he had it, he turned the reporter about, half supporting him, half leading him as he moved on wobbly legs. What happened between Cordovez and the driver, Jeff never knew, but as usual the little man handled his assignment with dispatch. By the time Jeff had pushed Spencer into the front seat, Cordovez appeared, lugging the heavy suitcase. Seconds later he was behind the wheel and gunning the motor, with Spencer beside him, while Jeff sat in back with Karen.

Once on the highway, Jeff reached down and opened the zipper on the flight bag. His fingers found the Manila envelope at once and when he began to probe the contents he could feel the packets of bills inside. He glanced ahead at Spencer, who was sitting up now, his gaze fixed on the windshield.

"This wraps you up, Spencer," he said.

"How does it?" the reporter said glumly.

"Harry Baker was killed for this money. You've got it."

"I didn't take it from Baker."

"Who did?"

"Luis Miranda."

"But you knew Miranda had it."

"Sure I knew it."

"Somehow Grayson also knew Miranda had it," Jeff said, trying to sort out the things he knew and the things he had heard. "He made Miranda return it yesterday afternoon. You knew that too." When there was no reply, he said: "You'd better make it good, Spencer; you haven't got much time."

There was still no answer and now Jeff tried to fit this new information into the bits and pieces already in mind.

The guess he finally made was well considered and proved to be accurate.

"You're the one who made that phone call."

"What phone call?"

"Someone called from Harry Baker's room the night he was killed at seven minutes after eight. The police assumed Baker had made the call until they discovered his spine had been shattered, which made a call like that impossible. You said Miranda took the money."

"He did."

"But he didn't make the call. I saw him out in front of the hotel," Jeff said. "He stopped to speak to my driver. When I got to the desk it was eight minutes after eight, so Miranda couldn't have been in Baker's room a minute earlier."

"Aye!" The word came from Cordovez accompanied by a slapping sound. The detective had clapped his palm to his forehead.

"What's the matter?"

"Julio Cordovez is an imbecile," the little man said. "Aye, to be so stupid . . . I have seen Luis Miranda come out," he said. "I told you I was waiting there at Señor Baker's instruction. I saw you arrive, and Miranda. But I also saw Miranda come from the hotel a minute earlier and put an envelope in his car. I never think this can be big enough to hold all that money. I do not think at all."

"You hear that, Lane?" Spencer said. "Satisfied?"

"That Miranda took the money, yes. But you made the call. You were in his room."

"All right," Spencer said resentfully, "I'll tell you. . . . Sure I was in the room. I knew about the payoff. Grayson had a lot of fun telling me. He said I'd been on his back for a weekly payment and now he was getting clean with Vegas and clearing out and he hoped I starved to death.

"I asked for the assignment at the hotel so I could see

what happened. I saw Grayson give the envelope to Baker. I was waiting when Baker came down later and left the key at the desk before he went into the bar, so I stepped up and palmed it. I went upstairs and started looking for the envelope and I hadn't hardly started when I heard somebody at the door. I just had time to duck into the closet when in walks Miranda. I can't figure why he wants the money but that's the way it is."

"Never mind," Jeff said as he remembered the reason Muriel Miranda had given him. "What's the rest of it?"

"He starts going through the drawers and comes up with this gun. He has it in his hand and is trying to pick the lock on the suitcase and Baker walks in on him."

"He'd come back to get his wallet," Jeff said.

"I guess so. Anyway, Miranda starts to apologize. He says he's in the wrong room, but Baker won't go for it. He don't know Miranda. To Baker the guy's a thief and he moves up and makes a grab for the gun and it goes off. Miranda takes his keys. He opens the suitcase and takes off with the envelope and I don't dare make a move because I know he'll plug me too."

He swore softly and took a breath. "There I am, maybe going to get mixed up in murder, and I haven't even got the dough. I don't know Baker couldn't make a call, so I take a chance. I dial Grayson's place and luckily I get him. I pretend I'm Baker. I say, 'Miranda's got the money,' and hang up."

Jeff believed this much as he recalled the session in Pedro Vidal's private office. Grayson had called Miranda before he came to *Segurnal*. But later the lawyer had walked out on him in spite of Grayson's annoyance.

"You figured Grayson would force Miranda to return the money," he said.

"I knew he would. He had to have the cash with this hotshot from Vegas in town. But I wouldn't stand a chance

of getting that envelope from Miranda. I had to stir up
some trouble and hope. I followed Miranda all the next
day," he said. "And at that you nearly loused it up for
me."

"How?"

"You were there, across the street. Miranda had to park
a couple of blocks away, but I had a cab. I knew where
he must be going so I was ahead of him. Remember when
I asked you to have a beer, how I swung you round so
your back was to the street? Well, if I hadn't, you'd have
seen Miranda go into the building. Boy, was that a break
when you turned down that beer?

"The minute you started down the street I went up there.
I hoped there'd be trouble that might give me a chance,
and there was. I inched the outer door open and Miranda
was beating the hell out of Grayson. I ducked behind the
door when he came out and when I went in again there
was Grayson dead on the floor and there was the envelope on the desk."

"Miranda didn't have any further use for it," Jeff said.

"I don't know about that," Spencer said. "All I know
is, it was there and I grabbed it and got out. I hotfooted
it to the office and shoved it under some papers in my desk
drawer."

Jeff snapped on the dome light and examined the envelope. The return address of Grayson Enterprises had
been printed in one corner. The top had been sealed and
three strips of Scotch tape had been added for security.
A hole had been torn in one side, but this had also been
taped shut.

Jeff began to work on the tape. It took him quite a while
before he had the envelope open but when he looked inside he could see the packets of orange-colored bills neatly
contained by paper bill straps. There were eight of these
and he picked up one of them, noting the figure on the

bill strap and the five-hundred-bolivar bills on top and bottom.

He riffled through that packet, stared, did it again. He sat back, dropping the bills back into the envelope. After a moment he swore softly and Karen Holmes stirred beside him and touched his arm.

"What is it, Jeff?" she asked. "It's the money, isn't it?"

"Yes," he said. "It's money all right."

"We are nearly there," Cordovez said. "We go to Miranda's?"

"We go to Grayson's."

Cordovez started to turn his head, thought better of it, and resumed his driving, swinging uphill a minute or two later and coming to a stop in the front of the familiar low-slung ranch house.

"You will want me?" Cordovez said.

"We'll all go," Jeff said, and led the way, with Spencer in front of him and Karen by his side.

He did not pay any attention to Cordovez, knowing that he was bringing up the rear. He did not bother to investigate the odd sound that came from behind as the door opened and Dudley Fiske registered his surprise. He saw Fiske move out of the way as Spencer advanced. Karen entered and so did he. Only then did he notice that Fiske had stepped back, that his bespectacled eyes held a startled look. By the time he turned to look behind him Carl Webb had the situation well in hand.

"Into the living-room," he said. "All of you."

Julio Cordovez had stopped just across the threshold. His chin had sagged and his expression was sheepish and embarrassed. His raised hands testified to the gun in his back, and as Jeff watched, Webb reached under the detective's coat and removed the revolver. He gave Cordovez a forward push and shouldered the door shut.

"O. K., little man," he said. "Find a chair somewhere and behave yourself."

21

DIANA GRAYSON had been sitting on the divan and she remained that way as her startled gaze assessed her callers and she began to understand what had happened. Fiske, still watching Webb, backed up and eased down beside her. Karen Holmes took a near-by chair and Jeff stood beside it, conscious now of the gun in his pocket and the envelope in his hand. Only Cordovez seemed utterly disconsolate as he watched Webb empty the shells from his revolver, snap the cylinder in place, and put it down on the table. When he put the shells beside it his hard-jawed face twisted in a grin.

"That makes us even, little man," he said. "You can collect it later."

Cordovez remained crushed. "I do not see him," he said to Jeff. "He must be in the bushes by the door. All I know" —he snapped his fingers—"I have this gun in my back."

"Forget it," Jeff said.

"Yeah," Webb added. "Let's have a look at that envelope, Lane. Maybe this will turn out to be my lucky day after all."

Jeff passed over the envelope and watched Webb back away to put it beside the empty gun.

"How come you were outside?" he asked.

"I couldn't figure out where the money could be," Webb

said. "I thought I'd hang around here awhile and maybe case the joint. Who had it?"

"Spencer." Jeff glanced at the reporter, who had dropped sideways onto the arm of an overstuffed chair and now presented an expression of acute melancholia. "We picked him up at the airport."

"Nice going." Webb glanced inside the envelope, grinned, and tucked it under his arm.

"You figure you can get out of the country with that?" Jeff asked.

"I can try. I haven't got too much to lose."

"Hadn't you better count it first?"

"Count it?" Webb eyed him suspiciously. He considered the others in the room. Then, to make certain he had not been the victim of some hoax, he held the envelope by one end and dumped the contents on the table. He picked up one packet, turned it over to reveal the five-hundred-bolivar note on either side. He inspected the figures on the bill strap.

"Eight bundles of fifty thousand B's each," he said. "That's fifteen grand U.S. Eight times fifteen is—"

"Take another look."

By that time Webb's irritation was showing and he did not hesitate. He bent the orange-colored top bill back and stared at the blue-green bill beneath. The figure on it was 10. He tried again; then riffled the rest of the money expertly. Satisfied now that he had a packet of ten-bolivar bills except for the five-hundred-bolivar notes on top and bottom, he looked up, his jaw rigid and his mouth ugly.

"What the hell is this?"

He grabbed a second packet and again discovered that it contained ten-bolivar bills except for the two five-hundred bills which covered them.

"Somebody pulled a switch," he said savagely. "Who? Come on, goddam it, who did it?"

Jeff had been watching the others. He saw the looks of surprise on Karen's face, on Cordovez's. Spencer was staring openmouthed and incredulous. Only Fiske and Diana Grayson presented the same stony-eyed calm.

"Ask Fiske," Jeff said. "He ought to know."

Webb advanced a step toward Fiske and the muzzle of the gun came up.

"Where's the rest of it?"

"In the bank." Fiske folded his arms, his bespectacled gaze steady, his voice controlled as he asserted his new-found maleness in front of the woman he loved. "And waving that gun isn't going to get it out, either," he said. "It's Diana's money, and unless you can crack the bank, it's going to stay there."

Webb's gun was steady and he still looked dangerous. Because Jeff wasn't sure what he might do, he stalled for time.

"How?" he said to Fiske. "How did you manage it? You knew Grayson had the cash. You knew he was going to pay off but—"

"Sure we knew." Fiske glanced at the woman. "Your stepbrother was the kind to brag about things like that. He raised the cash and he was pulling out. Diana could have the house for her share but that was all.

"He came back from the bank the day before yesterday with eight packs of five-hundred-bolivar bills—a hundred bills in each. He dumped them out on his desk. He wasn't worried about me. He never figured I had any guts—and he was right. He packed the bills in this company envelope, sealed it, fixed it up with Scotch tape, and locked it in his desk. What he forgot was that the key to my desk also fitted his."

He paused, not boasting, not even sounding proud of what he had done. He was simply reciting a tale that he himself found hard to believe even now.

"I don't know where I got the nerve," he said. "But when I thought about Diana"—he reached out to touch her hand—"and what Arnold was doing to her, I made up my mind I wasn't going to let him get away with it. I sent the girl out after he left, took the envelope and another like it and some Scotch tape, and went back to the bank. I had an account there and I got a lot of ten-B bills. I asked for some of those paper bill straps and then I went to one of those little rooms in the safe-deposit department and locked myself in.

"It took me about ten minutes to fix new bundles with ninety-eight tens and a five-hundred top and bottom. I taped the new envelope just like the old one. I put the rest of the five-hundreds in my safe-deposit box, came back to the office, and locked the envelope in his desk."

"You went to the hotel that night when Grayson delivered it to see what would happen," Jeff said.

"Right. I didn't think he'd count it again, not after sealing the envelope that way. I didn't think Baker would either, but I hung around outside looking up at Baker's room and watching the lobby from the pool entrance. If there'd been any trouble I would have known it."

"You knew Webb would count it," Jeff said.

"Sure."

"Naturally," Diana said, speaking for the first time. "But then it wouldn't matter. We thought probably when Mr. Webb found out the debt hadn't been paid he would come looking for Arnold. We knew Arnold couldn't raise that much money again, nor prove that Dudley had taken it. What happened between Arnold and Mr. Webb then was none of our concern."

The way she said it understated the problem and Jeff put it another way. "You mean if Arnold wound up on the side of the road with a couple of slugs in his head it wouldn't bother you."

"Frankly, no."

Jeff shook his head and swallowed. He believed all he had heard and, now that he understood this woman and what she had been through at the hands of his stepbrother, he was not particularly surprised. It was for Fiske and his new-found daring that he felt a certain grudging respect.

"That seems to be it, Webb," he said.

The man from Las Vegas had lowered his gun but he still looked puzzled. Apparently he had been doing some arithmetic, because he said:

"Christ, there's only about three grand U.S. here. Not even that."

"It'll pay your expenses," Fiske said, "and give you something for your time. You're welcome to it," he said. "So why don't you take it and start traveling? There'll be no beef from us, will there, Diana?"

Webb thought it over and considered the odds. Then, proving that as a gambler he could be a good loser, he stuffed the bills back into the envelope and stuck it under his arm.

"It was hardly worth the trip," he said. "But it's better than nothing and I guess you can't collect from a dead man or crack a bank." He backed to the entrance hall and glanced at Cordovez. "Take it easy with the gun, little man. Don't give me any trouble."

Jeff glanced at Spencer when the door closed. "I guess you didn't count it either."

The reporter still looked dazed. "All I did," he said, "was tear a hole in the envelope. When I saw those pretty orange-colored five-hundreds it was enough for me. Why should I count it?" he asked plaintively.

"Come on," Jeff said and nodded to Cordovez who had gone over to reload his gun. He touched Karen's arm. "We've got one more stop before *Segurnal*."

Luis Miranda acted as his own butler that evening. He opened the door himself after he had snapped on the overhead light, and when he recognized his callers, he bowed slightly and stepped back to let them enter. They waited in the hall until he had closed the door and then he led them into a long, impressive-looking room with a stained-beam ceiling and heavy curtains. The rug was thick, the furniture heavy but formal, and the two floor lamps which were lighted still left much of the room in shadow.

"Won't you sit down?" he asked politely.

Jeff thanked him and moved with Karen to a divan that looked comfortable but wasn't. Spencer selected an overstuffed chair and Cordovez took a straight-back at one side.

"Were you expecting us?" Jeff said.

"I was not sure. When the bell rang I thought it might be someone from *Segurnal*. You see, my wife told me about the riding crop she turned over to you. I was not sure what you would do with it."

"I can bring you up to date," Jeff said. "It may take quite a while—"

"I would like to hear what you have to say."

Jeff took a breath and began by speaking of Dan Spencer, the envelope he had taken, and the substitution that Fiske had made in Grayson's office. He explained how Spencer had taken Karen to Macuto, and how he had been picked up at the airport.

He paused here, but when there was no reaction from Miranda he went on to repeat Spencer's story of what had happened the night Harry Baker had been killed. When he finished he asked if Miranda had anything to add.

The lawyer's smile was thin and mirthless and his black eyes were fathomless in the shadows.

"Nothing at this time," he said. "I am an attorney, Mr. Lane, and I prefer to do my talking before a judge."

"You don't deny you took the money?"

"How can I deny it?"

"You wanted the money so Grayson could not pay off and go back to the States—with your wife. He found out you had it and threatened to go to the police unless you returned it. He did not care who had killed Baker, but he had to have the money. You took it back yesterday afternoon."

"That is quite true."

"You took the riding crop with you because that was the only way you could settle your account. You didn't care if he had you arrested or not."

"In this country, a man has the right to protect his home and his good name. When the truth was known, no judge would convict me for what I did to Arnold Grayson."

"Did you intend to kill him?"

"No. I wanted only to show my contempt, to let my wife see him. I could not prevent her leaving but I could perhaps make her understand what manner of man she had chosen." He paused and his voice grew quiet. "I did not know he was dead when I left," he said. "I did not think I had struck him hard enough. I only meant to—"

The word choked off abruptly and when Jeff glanced up he saw that Miranda's eyes had focused beyond him. Not understanding why, he looked at Cordovez and what he saw was even more disturbing. For the little man was sitting on the edge of his chair, his eyes wide open and staring. Something akin to fear was mirrored there and the sight of it triggered a nervous spasm that sent an icicle racing up Jeff's spine. When he jerked his head round and saw Muriel Miranda standing no more than five feet away, he froze that way, his gaze fastening on the little automatic she held in her hand.

The door through which she had come gave on the rear of the center hall and that part of the room lay in shadow.

How long she had been listening no one could say, for she had made no sound as she approached and the dark dress had served as protective coloring. Now, as she stopped, her face was white and rigid, the mouth a scarlet slash.

"So you did kill him," she said in a voice Jeff had never heard. "You lied," she said. "You told me you had only given him a thrashing. If he had not been dead, Spencer would not have dared to take the money."

Miranda faced her, his shoulders erect, his patrician face a brown mask in the lamplight. He looked immaculate in his slacks and blue dressing-jacket. Gold links gleamed from the long French cuffs of his silk shirt. He made no move and his voice was clear and controlled.

"If you heard me, you know I said I did not think he was dead. I still do not."

"I told you what I'd do, Luis."

She took another step and Jeff eased off the divan and got his feet under him, his throat tight and an odd fear expanding inside him.

"Wait a minute," he said. "That's not the way."

"Keep out of it," Muriel said.

"My stepbrother's not worth it," Jeff argued. He's not worth hanging for."

"They don't hang women here. They don't even hang men."

Jeff looked at her eyes then and what he saw told him that, for this moment at least, the woman was no longer sane. She had brooded too long over a pyramiding burden of injustice, real or fancied, and this new desire for vengeance had corroded her ability to accept the blow which had been dealt her plans for the future. She had been infatuated with an idea rather than a man, but the loss was no less real to her now.

In her present mood the capacity for murder was there

and Jeff knew that she might start pulling the trigger any minute unless someone stopped her. When he saw her hand tighten he spoke brusquely.

"You're just going to start shooting, is that it?"

"Yes."

"Because you think your husband killed Grayson."

"Yes."

"That would be a very bad mistake."

"What?"

"The way you're aiming that thing you'll kill the wrong man."

For the first time he had her attention. She looked at him, a gleam of recognition showing in the bright-blue eyes.

"What did you say?"

"What I'm trying to say is—I don't think your husband killed my stepbrother. I don't think he killed Baker."

"Then who did?"

"Dan Spencer."

He was watching the gun as he spoke. He thought the hand that held it wavered. He had planted the first small seed of doubt, but he had convinced no one.

"I don't believe you," she said huskily.

"Me?" Spencer jerked erect in his chair and his mouth was open. "Are you crazy?"

"I don't think so," Jeff said and edged sideways so that he came between Spencer and the gun.

22

FOR A long moment, then, no one spoke, no one moved. The silence built. The tension that followed began to stiffen the backs of Jeff's legs and his breath came shallowly. He had to keep talking. He had to be convincing. But even then he knew it might not be enough.

There were too many guns in the room. The one he had taken from Spencer was still in his pocket, but he was not equipped to use it with any great skill. What the woman might do when the truth came out there was no way of telling, and always there was Cordovez, the expert, who as yet had made no move. He sat at an angle to Spencer and it was the reporter who had his attention now rather than Muriel Miranda.

"What is this?" Spencer said, his amber eyes harried and uncertain. "I told you what I did."

"We heard you," Jeff said. "And most of it is true. You were in the closet in Harry Baker's room when Miranda took the money—but I think you made one switch."

He looked at Miranda, who seemed not to have moved a muscle. "You may not get a chance to talk to that judge," he said. "I think you'd better talk now. You'd better answer one question, and you'd better be right. Someone used the house telephone and called Baker's room at one minute after eight. Was it you?"

"Yes," said Miranda and his breath came out with the word.

"To make sure no one was in the room before you went up."

"Yes."

That was the answer Jeff needed and he went quickly ahead, the tension still with him but confident now that he had what he needed. He spoke mostly to Spencer, but from where he stood he could also watch the woman with the gun.

"Baker was already dead when Miranda went into the room. You were in the closet, all right, Spencer, and you saw him take the money. You didn't dare make a move, either, because it meant you'd be tagged for murder."

"That's what you say," Spencer said. "I say Baker was dead when I got there. Maybe you can prove he wasn't."

"I don't know what you mean by proof," Jeff said, "but I can give you some facts you may have forgotten. Follow me," he said. "See how they sound."

He swallowed and said: "Baker came down to the desk about ten minutes of eight and left his key. You admit you took it. He went into the bar and ordered a martini and then discovered he had forgotten his wallet. He went to the desk and got a duplicate key at about five minutes of eight and went to his room.

"I say he walked in on you instead of Miranda, who did not come until *after* one minute after eight. You're the one who had the gun you'd found in the drawer, and Baker, being the sort of man he was, tried to take it. He was shot close-up, so maybe the gun did go off in the struggle. I'm not saying you killed him deliberately, but—"

"You're not saying anything that makes any sense," Spencer said defiantly. "You've got nothing to back it up."

"I haven't finished," Jeff said. "But this much I know: a man who leaves a martini on a bar to go get his wallet would have only that one thing in mind: to get that wallet and come back for his drink. Baker went to his room but he didn't get the wallet. *It was still in the pocket of his other suit where Ramon Zumeta found it.* I say the reason he didn't get the wallet is because he ran into something in his room that stopped him.

"I say someone was there. Not Grayson, not Webb, not me, not Miranda who could have been there at that time. You, Spencer! You were there and you got trapped. You were still there a couple of minutes later when Miranda walked in on you." He looked at the lawyer. "How did you get in?"

"I got a key from a maid," he said. "Later I paid her handsomely to forget she had given it to me."

"Baker was dead?"

"Yes. I did not know how or why." He hesitated and his gaze dropped. When he continued his tone was embarrassed and uneven. "I had not done this but I knew I could be involved. But I was not thinking of that, but of Muriel and your stepbrother, and the money. I took the envelope from the traveling bag." He sighed heavily. "It was a great mistake. I know that now."

Spencer's sallow face was shiny and his defenses were cracking. His eyes had a hunted look and he had trouble keeping them still. All he had left now was bluster and he tried it again.

"That's not proof," he said nastily. "That's theory."

"It's sound, though," Jeff said. "And maybe there's more." He moved closer, his dark gaze intent and his mouth grim. "Grayson didn't die from the beating Miranda gave him. The report says he died from asphyxia." He glanced at Cordovez. "What about the coat, Julio?"

"As you suspected, there were bloodstains."

Jeff spoke of the jacket he had seen on the office floor. "I think you smothered him, Spencer. You sneaked in to get the money, thinking he was dead or unconscious, and he fooled you. He was in bad shape by that time, but he must have made a grab for you and you had to silence him. Maybe you didn't mean that either—not that it matters.

"The autopsy showed one more thing," he said. "Bloodstains and bits of tissue and fine hair under Grayson's fingernails. Stick your hands out," he said. "Let's see the backs of your hands and your wrists."

Spencer hesitated a moment, his gaze challenging. Slowly then, his manner as deliberate as it was defiant, he extended both arms, palms down. "Take a look," he sneered. "Go ahead."

Jeff could tell then that there were no marks here and that left him only one more chance. He took a breath and continued doggedly.

"O. K., Spence. But you were quite a sport-shirt guy when I first saw you. You had one on that night at the Tucan. You wore one when I saw you in front of Grayson's office, but that evening you had on a white shirt and a tie. Why, Spence? Because Grayson got one hand on your throat before you could quiet him?"

He was reaching for the reporter even as he spoke. He got his fingers inside the white shirt near the collar and yanked before Spencer could duck back.

Two buttons popped and the shirt came open as Spencer was half lifted from his seat. That left the hairy upper part of his chest exposed as it had been when Jeff first saw him in a sport shirt. It was much the same now except for the two inch-long scars that stood out vividly at the base of the throat.

Jeff let go of the shirt. He took one look at the sallow face. When it began to crumble he stepped back, his job was done and he felt all used up inside. For that instant he forgot the threat of death that still hovered over the room and what happened occurred so swiftly that he had no time to understand.

Intent on Spencer, he had his back to Muriel Miranda

and did not realize he no longer blocked her line of fire until he heard her cry out, a wild, despairing sound that shocked his nerve-ends and made his scalp crawl. Instinctively he wheeled and for that next instant time stood still. He saw the leveled gun, the contorted face, the blur of motion at one side as Miranda, who had moved much closer to his wife, struck hard at her wrist with the heel of his hand before she could fire at Spencer.

The gun went off as it spun from her fingers and she cried out in sudden pain. It hit the floor near Jeff's feet, skidded and bounced as he reached for it and missed. Then Spencer had scooped it up and was straightening on the edge of his chair, his gaze still frightened, but with dangerous glints in the amber eyes where none had been before.

Jeff took a backward step as he stared into the muzzle. He glanced at Cordovez, who had not yet moved. He looked over at Karen who sat white-faced and still on the divan, her eyes round with shock and amazement. Finally he looked at Miranda.

He had his arm around his wife now, his face close to hers. He spoke soft words that no one else could hear and now, as reaction hit her and sanity returned, her eyes had a dazed look, and she whimpered like a little child while she massaged her wrist.

"You hurt me," she said, her face slack as she let herself be led to the divan.

When he had his emotions in hand, Jeff considered Spencer. He remembered things Carl Webb had said. A mouse who would never fight back unless cornered, and too fast on his feet for that.

The gun made the difference. For Spencer had killed twice, not with premeditation but because he had been trapped. He was still trapped. He was still afraid, his amber eyes said so. But that did not make the threat less real. And so, because he could think of nothing else at the moment, Jeff began to talk.

"Why did you smother Grayson?" he asked in a voice that was hard to keep steady.

"He grabbed me." Spencer wet his lips and one hand moved absently to the scars at the base of his throat. "I thought he was unconscious. The envelope was on the desk. I had my back to him and he grabbed my ankle."

He swallowed and said: "I came down on top of him and the chair came with me. He rolled free and tried to get the gun from the desk and I knocked him back and then he started to yell. I—I guess I panicked. I grabbed the coat. I tried to shut him up and he grabbed my throat. I held the coat over his face. I put my weight on it. I had to."

"And what are you going to do with that?" Jeff said, indicating the gun.

"If somebody makes a move I'm going to use it. I've got to get away."

"Where? Your only chance would be the back country and you wouldn't last a week."

"I could lock you all up. That would give me time. There must be a place."

He said other things but Jeff no longer heard him. For just then some movement caught the corner of his eye. He controlled the impulse to shift his gaze but he knew that Cordovez's hand had slipped unnoticed inside his jacket, and now his stomach was suddenly tight and he stood immobile, the perspiration drying coldly on his spine.

For he felt instinctively that with a gun Cordovez was not only expert but deadly. Once Spencer tried to use that little automatic he would be a dead man, and though the reporter had little courage, he could panic. It was not that Jeff felt any great sympathy for him. Spencer had been a victim of avarice and circumstance. He had killed, but not viciously or with malice. Jeff could not stand there

and watch him die, nor did he dare make a warning gesture lest Cordovez be the victim when Spencer sensed his
peril. And so, because there was no other way, he fell back
on reason and his knowledge of the reporter's character,
his voice blunt, impatient, and hard.

"Be smart for once, Dan," he said. "You can't handle
this one. It's too big for you and you know it. Nobody can
accuse you of murder with premeditation, and this is not
the States, you can't hang here. There's a penalty you'll
have to pay, but fight it out in court and take your chances.
What are his chances, Miranda?" he asked. "What could
he expect?"

The lawyer was watching Spencer. "You would do well
to follow that advice," he said. "You are still a young man
and a few years at San Juan de los Morros in our model
prison should not be too difficult. I once made an offer to
Mr. Lane," he said. "It was not in good taste but I meant
it. I told him if he was arrested I would defend him without charge. I will do the same for you, to the best of my
ability, because you have done me a favor by removing
Grayson, who was an evil man. Perhaps"—his glance
strayed to the woman beside him, though she seemed not
to hear—"you have given me a second chance."

Spencer had been listening and the gun shifted in his
hand. Fundamentally he had no heart for killing. He had
always chosen the easiest way and he wavered now.

"How many years?" he said.

Miranda shrugged. "I cannot promise, but I can tell you
this. In my country there are no juries. It is the judge who
decides, and often pressure is brought to bear which can
influence him. The heaviest penalties come as a result of
the pressure brought by the family and relatives of the
victim who wish vengeance. I do not know about Baker,
but with Grayson I do not believe there will be any such
pressure."

He glanced again at Jeff to see if he would deny this. "With no one to cry out for vengeance and no one to care, I would say"—he tipped one hand—"perhaps five years, considering the circumstances. But this I promise you: there will be no defense by me unless you put down that gun, and at once."

Spencer took a great shuddering breath and his mouth trembled. He looked down at the gun. Then, as though knowing in his heart that he had neither the courage nor the ability to fight alone for very long, he reached out and put the gun on the table.

Jeff felt his knees weaken and he leaned against the edge of the divan to support himself. For he was watching Cordovez now and knowing what a close thing it had been.

"You don't know how lucky you are," he said in shaky tones.

"Lucky?"

Spencer frowned, brows warping. He hesitated and then, held by something in Jeff's face, he turned to see what Jeff was looking at.

Cordovez, hunched slightly in his chair, sat very still. One hand had slipped inside his open jacket and the gun was there, the muzzle pointed right at Spencer's hollow chest. Slowly then the hand relaxed and Spencer understood completely how death had been waiting for him while he made up his mind.

It may have been this that caused the reaction. It may have been a cumulative process brought on by the realization that everything he had tried had turned out badly, that even the envelope he had tried so hard to run away with proved in the end to have little value. Whatever the reason, he seemed to shrink back in the chair as his mouth opened. A sobbing, convulsive sound tore at his throat and suddenly he put his face in his hands and doubled up, rocking back and forth as his self-control disintegrated and his emotions took charge.

Jeff turned aside, unable to watch any longer. He saw Cordovez replace his gun and step over to take the automatic Spencer had discarded.

"Thank you," the little man said. "I did not know what to do. When hysteria touches a man there is no telling what might happen."

"Yeah," Jeff said. "Yeah." Then, when he found more words: "Will you call *Segurnal?* You can talk to them better than I can."

Cordovez glanced round until he located the telephone. When he dialed, Jeff looked at Miranda, who now sat silently beside his blond wife. Her face still showed traces of shock and her eyes were closed, but she made no resistance when he took her hand and pressed it between his own.

"Spencer was not the only one who was lucky," he said as Jeff moved up to sit beside Karen.

He started to take her hand and found his palms wet. He took out a handkerchief and wiped them and then she took it away from him and wiped his forehead. When he retrieved it he kept her hand and found that he could smile.

There were a million things he wanted to say and there was no place to start. The dark-blue eyes were watching him closely now and her smile was sweet and suddenly he knew that what had to be said could much better be said tomorrow or the next day or the day after that.

There would be plenty of time and so he leaned back beside her, his shoulder touching hers while the strain and the worry began to drain slowly from his body. Somewhere in the distance he heard Julio Cordovez chattering in excited Spanish, but he did not listen. For the moment he was content to sit unthinking beside this girl who understood his mood and made no demands of her own. They were still there three minutes later when the first of the radio cars arrived.

A NOTE ON THE TYPE

The text of this book is set in Caledonia, a Linotype face designed by W. A. Dwiggins, the man responsible for so much that is good in contemporary book design and typography. Caledonia belongs to the family of printing types called "modern face" by printers—a term used to mark the change in style of type-letters that occurred about 1800. It has all the hard-working feet-on-the-ground qualities of the Scotch Modern face plus the liveliness and grace that is integral in every Dwiggins "product" whether it be a simple catalogue cover or an almost human puppet.